Viking Mania

Selected Stories of Kings and Queens, Gods and Ghosts

Robert Peterson

Illustrated *by* Kory Fuhrman

St. Wilfrid Press

St. Wilfrid Press

Miami

Printed in the United States of America

First eBook Illustrated Edition 2022

Library of Congress 2022906701

ISBN -13 978-0-578-29008-9

This book is dedicated to
Drs. Arnold Ghitis, Kevin Ergle,
Lea Harracksingh and
Karen Brittain, RN, MSN,
whose combined efforts did
so much to restore my health

Contents

Preface

Storytelling among the Norse is considered an art. Probably one developed of necessity when you think of the long and often cheerless winters they had to endure. Few were the grandmothers who didn't have a rich store of these stories to entertain both old and young. Many of these stories are violent by modern standards, but the world was a very different place back in the dim ages following the fall of Rome. This was a time when public executions were common and gruesome, and all too many people knew firsthand what wars, famine, and pestilence could do.

Many of these tales centered on monsters and other terrifying creatures that stalked the darkened hills or lived under bridges, all the while waiting to devour or otherwise torment their victims. In the gloom of winter on a remote farm, it was easy to believe that such creatures existed, so it follows that this sort of story can be found in great numbers. Indeed, many a child went to bed very concerned about being visited by a troll, a goblin, or an ill-tempered fire-breathing dragon.

But there are other stories as well, often having to do with fate and the will of the Gods. Yet the Gods can be fickle and destiny hard to fathom, leading to stories in which fate is ultimately borne out but only in baffling circumstances.

Bravery in battle and loyalty to one's comrades are also grist for the storyteller's mill, as are the tales concerning famous kings and their families and morality stories in which virtuous maidens are put in tough spots. Here follows a sample of stories that might be told by a grandparent or an aged warrior as the generations sat around the fire on a cold winter night.

Chapter One

The Saga of Harefoot Grimisson

People Didn't Mourn His Death

There was a boy who lived just outside a village on the border between the Blue Mountains and the Salmon River. His name was Lagerif, but everyone called him *Harefoot* because he could run so fast. He was the eldest son of Grim, who was a farmer and raider. His mother, Gunhildi, was kin to Torkvole the Red, who ruled the East Goths. Harefoot was bigger and stronger than most lads his age, but unlike others, he never cried or shed a tear. No matter if he was hurt in the rough play that boys like so much, or in a sport like wrestling, or even when he was beaten for bad behavior by his father, he never made a sound. The most that he would do in such circumstances was to wrinkle his nose and utter dark curses asking the All-Father to flay his enemies alive; he said this under his breath, of course.

Every year there was a celebration in honor of the wonderful kings that ruled the East Goths in olden times. Their descendants would put their statues on display in the village square where the rest of the people honored them (no matter if they wanted to or not) by placing beautiful flowers next to these wooden statues and loudly blessing the merciful kings of a bygone era. People who neglected to honor the kings of old had their tongues nailed to those same statues for a day or two.

Harefoot entered a swimming contest held at the river. The prize was a silver cup filled with coins. Indeed, he did swim very fast, but he was slowed when another boy bit his arm. Fighting while swimming was not against the rules, but Harefoot took great offense at being bitten, which was generally frowned on as *dirty fighting*. Later that day, during the archery competition, a sport he was not so good at; he accidentally made a shot that skewered that same boy's ass cheeks with a single arrow. Everyone laughed as the blood flowed down the lad's legs except his parents, who thought Harefoot had done this on purpose. That night, Harefoot and his parents strongly suspected their beer had been pissed in at the feast. But the innocent fun of the East Goths came to an end for the season; everyone returned home to take up their usual pursuits. Yet there was bad blood between the two families after this year's celebration.

Harefoot's reputation suffered another blow later in the year during the mid-winter celebration, where the Goths would feast and offer sacrifices to the Gods of Winter. He consulted a soothsayer in the hall of his uncle, who was a great landowner in those parts. He asked about his future; after looking at his palms and ear lobes and tasting the blood from a prick in his finger, she declared that his temper would be his undoing. For this, he whacked her face so hard with his hand as to split both her lips, and then he pulled a handful of hair out of her head for good measure. Some of the people who witnessed this incident began to wonder about him.

The following year Harefoot had just turned sixteen when the annual games began. He was by now almost a full-grown man; in fact, he towered over the other farm lads his age. He won the swimming competition easily by a large margin, and everyone expected him to win the wrestling contest too. But nobody told this to his opponent, whose brother had been shot in the arse by Harefoot the year before. He made up in skill for what he lacked in size; he flung Harefoot around like a girl's rag doll before pinning him to the earth. Humiliated, Harefoot stalked away from this discomfiture with a dark face while muttering terrible oaths of vengeance upon the boy who beat him. A man in the crowd, feeling sorry for Harefoot, handed him a hatchet as a gift to console him. But Harefoot refused to be comforted; instead, he chose to turn around, walk back to the victor, and bury the hatchet in the top of the boy's head. This happened so fast that almost nobody knew for sure what had happened. During the cries and yells of horror and grief, later replaced by mayhem as the families fought each other, Harefoot stole a horse and rode away. For stealing the horse, he was later declared at the All-Thing to be an outlaw and banished from the land of the Goths.

He raided for five years, eventually getting his own ship and crew. He was greatly feared for his ruthlessness and cunning; of course, he became very rich. When he was allowed to return home again, his family held a great feast in his honor. Harefoot was filled to overflowing with pride and haughtiness at his triumphant return. In a drunken state, he pounded the table with this fist, overturning mugs of beer, and spitefully insulted his father by saying that he could never understand how such an insignificant man had ever sired a great man as he. His father, angered, struck him a blow across the face with his fist so hard that Harefoot spat out a tooth. This enraged him so much that he turned red, then purple, then dead. He had died in a fit of anger at his father. He sat in his chair at the head of the table, eyes wide open, face blotched and bloated and very dead. Many of the folk who attended the feast ran forth, calling upon the Gods to witness that they had nothing to do with this matter.

A few days after his death, his family and friends put Harefoot's body in a grave across the field. Of course, very few lamented his death, but for the sake of the family's reputation, they were forced to place various goods in his grave, kill some animals to accompany him, and raise a mound over his corpse.

Most people preferred Harefoot dead as he only caused trouble when alive. They looked forward to forgetting that he ever lived while they went on with their toil-filled lives; unfortunately, there was little peace to be had in the coming weeks.

Four days later, the remains of a neighboring farmer were found torn apart in a field near his home. His wife said he had gotten up at night to find out why the horses were restive. He was sensible enough to carry an axe with him, yet his detached arm showed him still clutching the weapon that did him no service. This both mystified and terrified the populace.

Nobody could even think of what animal had done this; few believed mythological creatures such as trolls and werewolves existed. Many pates were scratched, and beards pulled as people strove to understand what had happened. Needless to say, the rust was rubbed off axes and swords as people took precautions. Doors were double barred; livestock was locked in barns at night. Amulets against enchantment were worn by just about everyone and placed over the household entrance.

But the attacks continued; the next victim was an old widow whose house was so solid it was like a small fortress, yet the door was torn off the hinges. Her remains were scattered all over, a foot was found in a nearby tree, and a half-eaten kidney was across the road. The Jarl was sent for; he came with his men and searched the area. At first, he thought maybe a troll had come down from the mountains as happened in the old tales; yet he was told that there were no such footprints as a troll would leave on the ground. He sent his son down the river with orders to tell the King all that had transpired; that evening, he stood to watch with a dozen picked men, but nothing happened.

Three days later, murder came to the house that Harefoot had been raised in. Somebody had smashed the stout oaken door at night and killed his parents, whose body parts were strewn wildly about. There was evidence that the old man fought with his sword, but none could say if he had in any way hurt his attacker. The house was so broken, smeared, and defiled by blood that the Jarl ordered the house burned forthwith. The people who lived in the nearby village and on the farms in the area wrung their hands in despair. Many would have fled if they had a place to go.

Then came a man to the village sent by the King, Jarl Eriksson, the King's younger cousin, with a troop of men on horses. He was a young man, yet he was clear-headed and shrewd. He talked to many people, old and young, high and low, man, woman, and crone. He asked searching questions about burials, especially recent ones. That night he sat in a tree near the mound of Harefoot Grimisson; he did the same the following night. Then he sent word to the farms near the burial mound to come at midday with shovels.

He ordered the body of Harefoot dug up and examined. At the murmurs of curses protecting the grave and the impropriety of digging up the dead, he said that any who did not lift a shovel would take Harefoot's place in the mound; everyone dug hard.

After a bout of furious digging done under the watchful eye of Jarl Eriksson, the body was uncovered. It showed no sign of decay but was strangely bloated with blood that leaked out of its nose, ears, and mouth. It was so heavy that it took six stout men to carry it out of the mound; the Jarl ordered it to be placed on a pile of logs and burned; then he stood to address the people.

"Last night, I sat in yonder tree," he said, pointing to an oak tree close by, "and kept watch. Just before dawn, I heard a loud noise as the earth opened up a path to the center of this mound. A creature, the one you see before you, came forth. It scared my horse so much that the animal broke loose from where I had tied him and ran off. This foul creature ran after it so fast that he almost caught him. Indeed, chasing my horse probably spared somebody's life.

This creature is an *afterwalker*, a cursed soul filled with an unholy rage and hatred that refuses to go to the underworld where it belongs. It has to be back in the ground before daylight, so I think it ran out of time in the vain pursuit of my horse. I saw it return and witnessed the earth swallow him up and shut behind him like a gate. This loathsome beast lived an unnatural life, feasting on the living for a time anyway. It cannot digest the bodies it consumes because it is dead, so it gets heavier and heavier until it is either killed or sinks into the grave too heavy to ever get out. I was fortunate that before I came here, I consulted a priest who was visiting from Uppsala who knew such things. Now we must burn the beast and dump his ashes in the ocean." The body was duly burned, and the ashes were disposed of. No more were the East Goths troubled at night by a fiend with an unruly temper.

Chapter Two

The Story of Thorstan the Thin

Odin Hears His Prayer

There was a man who was born in the village of Blat in Finland during the time of Yingelby the Usurper. His name was Thorsten, son of Elk the Scruffy. He was, as a lad, quite lean, so he came to be called *the thin*. This name, however, became an ironic name because when he became an adult, he was prone to excessive stoutness.

For the first part of his life, Thorsten worked on his uncle's farm. From an early age, he was sensitive to any critical comments about his lineage. Yet it was a matter of fact that his father (when young) had once been disciplined by the local jarl for having sexual congress with a goat in public. His mother had problems, too; she had (also when young) been expelled from the brothel she worked in for theft and immoral behavior. From such parents came this youth of great promise.

One day when he was a lad, he aided an old woman who was having trouble loading some bags of meal onto her wagon. She thanked him for his help but lamented the fact that she had no money to reward him with. Yet she offered to read his future for him saying that she had come from a long line of seers. He agreed and showed her his palm. She looked at it for a good long while before letting go. "You'll be a king someday, I know not where, but you will wear a crown." At this, he laughed as he knew that a low-born poor boy would never reach such heights. Yet she replied that such was his destiny, no matter if he thought so or not.

Like many young men, he wished to prove himself by raiding, so he joined his jarl's fleet of three ships. However, the jarl was in decline; old and sotted, he should never have put to sea. After only a few days out, they hit a dense fog causing him to make a terrible mistake in navigation. By the time he and his ships cleared the fog, they had gotten so lost that instead of sailing up a river to ravish a settlement of Swedes, he ended up attacking the heavily armed Cours, who have a reputation for exceptional ferocity. The few survivors of that raid were sold into slavery except for Thorsten, who managed to jump into the water and cling to a log long enough to escape.

While he managed to evade the anger of the Courlanders, his troubles were far from over. There was only one direction to flee and that was east. Here he had to cross rivers and streams where he was menaced by wild creatures. Giant snakes attempted to have him for lunch in stinking, muddy swamps. At night when he slept in trees, strange creatures called out, roared, or yelped in the dark. For food, he had only raw frog legs and eggs stolen from birds' nests. Day after day, he suffered as insects attempted to dine on his scrawny hide. Then the wildlands gave way to cultivation. Hope rose in his bosom that civilization of the sort that could help him was now in sight. He staggered into the first village he came to with eyes almost swollen shut from insect bites. Between his cracked and parched lips, he croaked out a plea for help. His cries attracted attention, but it was not precisely the kind that he was looking for.

He spent the night in a jail which was the most comfortable abode that he'd had in weeks, with water to drink that was at least clean. The coarse bread was hard to chew, but at least it had hardly any mold on it. So that night, for the first time in weeks, he slept in peace. But the next morning, he was taken out of his cell, his hands tied in front of him, and he was frog-marched to the center of the city. Here he noticed that he was not among humans but elves! This terrified him, for elves were known to be ill-natured with little love for humans.

He has hauled in front of an elf who could only be their king, where he was pushed down to his knees. The King stood in front of him dressed in long royal robes of red with black trim; upon his head was a great crown topped with egret feathers. He scowled down at the prisoner and demanded to know why this stinking varmint was being put into his royal presence.

"We found him spying, your majesty." Said the guards; the king ordered the prisoner to stand and then asked him several questions about where he came from, his family, and how he came to these parts. After Thorsten explained these things as clearly as he could, the King declared that he didn't believe a word of what was said. He then kicked the poor man's arse. The guards, acting on the universal precept that whoever royalty kicks, they too should kick, plied their feet energetically to his backside; in a matter of minutes, the poor prisoner's butt was too sore to sit even if he was offered a chair, which he wasn't.

"I'll give this matter some thought the King said as he stroked his hairless chin, "in the meantime, hang him." In vain did Thorsten plead for his life. But alas, when the rope was fetched, he knew that his time was all but over. In desperation, he called upon Odin, the All-Father, the Lord of the Gallows.

Odin, sitting in his chair within the walls of his fortress at Asgard, was busy hearing the news of the world from his ravens when came the desperate plea of Thorsten. Usually, he ignored such calls, but as this man was about to be hung by the elves, a race against whom he had a grievance; he took himself to the gallows disguised as a small dog.

With a great cheer, the elves at spear point made Thorsten climb a ladder where the hangman waited to put a rope around his neck. But when Thorsten reached the top of the ladder, it broke, spilling him and the hangman to the ground. A new ladder was brought, which was sturdier, for it easily held the weight of them both. The hangman put the noose around his neck, climbed down the ladder, and turned it on its side, flinging Thorsten into the air. He hung there for only a brief moment before the rope broke. Thorsten found himself sitting on his poor, abused rump below the tree branch. At this, the crowd grew restless; many began to walk away, thinking that there was magic at work here. One of those who left was the hangman. The King, who had witnessed these things, was filled with rage that his orders had been frustrated. He stomped his foot in anger as he shook his fist to the sky, thinking rightly that the God of the Gallows was responsible for this outrage.

"I'll walk to Hel on foot before I let this man escape. I am a powerful King; I won't be robbed of my justice by some old man who has only one eye. I'll be hanged myself before I let this filthy bugger live."

He then ran to the tree, where he picked up the ladder from the ground and leaned it against the tree. Joining the broken ends of the rope together with a knot, he forced Thorsten at knifepoint up the ladder for the third time. As the King mounted the rungs, he railed at his men for being cowards. He had a difficult time with the noose, though; he had condemned others to be hung often enough he had never done the work himself. By his clumsiness, he managed to entangle himself in the noose. Thorsten, seeing his chance, pushed the ladder away from the tree with his foot causing it to fall. Thorsten reached the ground, but the King did not. For quite a while, the King kept up a furious dance as he hung in the air between Midgard and Asgard. His efforts to grab the rope became feebler until, at last, his tongue, now blue, hung limply out of his mouth. The next day his minions cut the body down and threw it into the river; for while the King was feared while he was alive, he was not loved when he was dead.

The elves seeing that the Gods had punished their king while rewarding this stranger, chose him to be their King. Thorsten replied that he was not worthy of such a position, but they ignored his reticence crowning him with great pomp and ceremony. When over time, after a long rule over the elves, he died, he was remembered as *King Thorsten the Good*.

Chapter Three

The Tale of Einar and Odin's Spear

An Untrusty Elf Gets His Comeuppance

There lived a youth on a remote farm at the far end of Hunland named Einar Evenson; he was the only son of a couple who owned a small farm. One day a traveler brought news of the death of a relative who lived in the Vestfold. Since the deceased had no children, it was apparent that Einar's father would inherit the estate, but he was too old to travel, so Einar packed up his few possessions and set out to claim his family's inheritance.

On the road, he met an old man dressed in a long gray cloak and wearing a peculiar wide-brimmed, low-crowned hat that matched the color of his cloak. The man had a long beard and carried a staff; he was poor, for his robe was held around him not by a proper belt but by a rope. Einar felt sorry for the old man, so he shared his bread with him.

The old man told Einar that his name was Herran and that he lived by going from farm to farm, sharpening farm implements and weapons. He claimed to have in his possession a sharpening stone of magical properties; once it touched the blade, the metal would become sharp with an edge that would last for years. As proof of this, he took the youth's blade, an ancient hunting knife as blunt as a pig's snout and sharpened it. Einar thanked him heartily, but within a few days, he became suspicious about the old man, for he noted that sometimes he looked tired and frail, yet at other times he seemed exceptionally strong and fit. He also noted that the old man had good vision, which was unusual for somebody of his great age.

Early one morning, as they rose to refresh themselves from a nearby stream, a gang of thieves came upon them. But when they found that the two had no money, they resolved to kill them. Dead men, they knew, were much less likely to report their location and numbers to the authorities. Before they could do that, however, the old man asked if they had any weapons that needed sharpening. He explained to them his occupation of sharpening blades and showed them the whetstone that he had in his pocket. This they agreed to as none of their blades had a proper sharpening for quite some time. They could always kill them later, the robbers reasoned.

They took the old man and Einar to their camp deep in the woods that the robbers had made into their lair. There the old man showed his skill in the sharpening of blades. Indeed, the robbers had never seen the like of these sharp weapons. Eventually, they were left with only two robbers as guards; the others had left to patrol a nearby road where they hoped to find more victims. This did not turn out well, though, for the two men left as guards.

The old man then engaged the guards in conversation, showing them the proper way to sharpen a blade. He used one of their knives to show the proper method to be used. When he was done, he said that he would give this magical stone to whoever could jump the highest for it. Then he quickly threw it into the air. Before they could think, the men went leaping after it, only to taste his blade on the way down. Both men were dead before their bodies hit the ground. Einar was amazed at this, so much he could hardly stand, yet he said nothing. Before leaving, they took bags of food, weapons, and a kettle of beer. Then they made haste wishing to go as many miles as possible before the robbers returned.

Once they found the main road, they made good time as they continued westward. Einar noted that the old man never seemed to tire as he walked, yet Einar's own feet began to burn him as the afternoon began to wane. He was glad when he and Herran came to the home of a jarl. It was the custom for all jarls to offer hospitality to travelers. There were many buildings on this large farm, including, as always, a hall for feasting. They headed for the hall, of course, because visitors must make themselves known. But the old man dissuaded him from going right into the hall, saying that a guest should always sit by the woodpile in front and wait to be noticed; since Einar had never traveled before, he knew but little of manners, so he allowed himself to be guided by the more experienced man. After a short wait, a servant came to them, whereupon the old man made their needs known. He also volunteered to sharpen their farm tools and knives as a way to earn his food. He took out his whetstone from his pocket as proof of his words. Einar had never seen the stone up close before, so he regarded it closely. It was about the size of the palm of his hand and looked like any common stone of that sort, yet Einar noted that there were no marks on it. This confounded him, for he had seen with his own eyes the old man sharpening tools and blades with it.

The old man's offer to sharpen tools was met with instant approval as farm implements and kitchen knives, too, are more often than not dull. Soon the old man was seated on a tree stump with a pile of scythes at his feet, all dull to the point of being useless. Maids took him blades from the kitchen, and a few men brought out swords and axes to be ground. The old man liked his work for he sang a song as he worked. Einar heard the words to the song, but he could not understand the words. Yet apparently, animals did, for soon several dogs were seated near the old man as he worked and sang. Even a woodchuck came out of his hole to hear the melody. Einar was about to inquire about this strange language when they were summoned to the hall by a ringing bell, so he never found out what he was hearing.

That day the Jarl had been holding a court to decide the fate of a man who was a robber. Einar thought it possible that this man was a member of the same gang that had captured them earlier. The punishment was a foregone conclusion, as robbers were always hung. Indeed, Einar was told that anyone brought to trial was punished, often by hanging. The Jarl didn't believe in trying innocent people; that made no sense to him whatsoever.

Everyone on the estate was summoned for the hanging; the Jarl believed that witnessing a hanging had a salubrious effect on the populace. As soon as everyone was gathered, the bound man was brought forward, his name given along with the offense. He was given a last chance to speak, which he declined. The hangman, who chopped wood and caught rats when not employed as such, took the wretch to a large overhanging tree branch that served as rude gallows. There he forced him to stand on a barrel as the noose was put around his neck. Then the barrel was kicked away. Einar was sickened to see the man's legs dance as his face turned blue. Soon it was over, though; the man swung gently in the breeze, his tongue hanging obscenely out of his mouth. The assembled workers, who'd all seen such things before, slowly drifted away.

They took this opportunity to go to a nearby stream to wash. The old man shared a piece of soap with Einar that speedily removed the caked-on dirt from their journey. The powerful soap also began to remove the top layer of skin, which made the young man hop like a toad in a frying pan. The old man laughed at this. He lathered his body from head to toe; he was impervious to the effects of the strong soap. Later he told Einar that the reason that the soap did such a good job at removing dirt was that it was made from the bile of a badger mixed with lye. The old man might not have felt any ill effects from using that soap, but poor Einar suffered greatly from raw spots for several days after being scalded with the soap of great strength.

On the way back to the hall, the bell was rung, signaling that it was time for supper. Einar was eager to get his seat at the table for he was very hungry, but his companion restrained him. As the others made haste to go inside, the old man walked over to where the man who had been hanged was gently turning in the mild breeze. To his astonishment, he put his left hand on the dead fellow's brow while reciting words in a strange language. Then he saw the dead man's eyes open which almost made Einar shit his pants. For several minutes they stood there, Herran mumbling words in that strange dialect into the dead man's ear, then waiting for a silent reply. A short time later, this unnerving conversation was completed. Herran led the way to the meal as if nothing had happened; Einar had such a fright that he almost swallowed his tongue; he walked to the hall with great difficulty.

They left the hall as soon as they finished eating, which was fine with Einar, who was wearied by the events of the day. But before he lay down for his evening rest, Herran bid him to be ready for an early start. It would not be wise, he offered, to be anywhere near here when the sun rose.

Both men were very quiet when they rose from their pallets of straw the next morning. It was the cold hour before dawn when they crept out of the front gate past the sleeping guard. As they walked by the hanging corpse, the old man greeted it like he would a friend on his way to market. This, of course, put a chill in Einar's bowels. However, they did not manage to leave the farm unscathed, for they were hardly out of the gate when the dogs came panting after them. One of them bit Einar's ankle before the old man chased off the hounds with the end of his staff. He was not seriously injured, but his ankle took days to heal.

An hour later, as the sun was just showing itself over the horizon, Herran told Einar the reason that they had left so early. According to the dead man, who was indeed a robber, the jarl of this place had the bad habit of seizing strangers and then selling them as slaves. He would not fetch much, he said, but Einar would have sold for a good amount of silver as a field hand. That was part of the information that he got from the dead man. The other information concerned a mysterious elf that seemed to have the power to make himself invisible.

Einar asked him how anyone could remain invisible unless, of course, it was a magical spell. Herran, however, told him that while it did indeed involve magic, it was more than just a spell, for it involved a special cape that, when worn, would make the one wearing it invisible. This was accomplished by the weaving of thread spun from the sighs of maidens, the laughter of babes, and the cooing of doves. He said there was only one person in all of creation that could do that, and that was Volthir the elf. But the elf was hard to find, although many looked for him. The reason was that the elf often took gold and silver in payment for magical items but didn't live up to his part of the bargain. There were many among the Gods and men who were on the lookout for this treacherous elf. From what Herran learned from the hanged man, the robbers had been watching the elf for quite some time. They expected that he had a store of gold as elves often have. This was undoubtedly true, and if this was the elf Volthir the supply of gold was probably quite large. But there was only one way to find out, and that was to go to where the elf had been spotted.

This involved a walk of many miles until they came to a trail that led between a swamp and a forest. They followed the path with the old man frequently stopping to examine the ground. At length, they came to a narrow wooden bridge that crossed a stream some ways below. This interested Herran to no end as he walked to and fro, casting his eyes upon the trail. He then took some branches from a pine tree that he used to wipe the ground with as if he was using a rude broom. He had Einar hide behind some bushes at one end of the bridge while he hid behind a pine tree on the other side. There they would sit quietly, waiting for the elf. Even if he were wearing the cloak, his footprints would be seen in the dirt as he walked toward them. Then as he reached the narrow bridge, they would jump him. Between the two of them, the elf would be caught.

So it was that they spent a good part of the day lying in wait for the elf. The young man wasn't sure that catching an elf was a good idea, but he was reluctant to argue with a man who could talk to the dead. Towards the end of the afternoon, they heard a whistling sound coming down the trail. They heard it plain enough but saw nothing until prints began to appear on the freshly swept ground in front of the bridge. When he judged that the tracks had reached the bridge, the youth jumped out and leaped upon where he thought the elf might be. At the same time, Herran jumped out with a yell on the other end.

For a long minute, all was chaos as the elf struggled and fought the efforts of the two men to capture him. He almost broke free when he knocked the younger man off the bridge into the stream below. But the old man was too quick for him. The elf was pulled off the ground as he was taken by the scruff of his neck. Here he kicked and screamed as his cloak fell onto the ground revealing him clad in the bright red garments that elves are so fond of.

"Who dares to take me from my magical cloak? Who is it that wants to have their brains fried by my magical powers? Let me go now, or I will burn your eyes out with flames of dragon breath."

"Who dares to take you? I do, for I am Herran, the Whisperer of the Gallows Meat. Long ago, I paid your price for a magical weapon, but you cheated me. Now you will make good on your promise, or it will be you who will be roasted." At this, the elf stopped his fighting and hung his head. He knew that he had been bested and that he must now make good his previous agreement. He admitted as much to the old man, who was now engaged in looking around for his young accomplice, who he found in the creek below looking very much worse for wear. For he had fallen among the sharp stones that littered the side of the stream; when he reached out for a rock to steady himself on as he got up, the rock turned out to be a mother turtle who objected strenuously to being interrupted as she gave swimming lessons to her young offspring. She clamped down on his hand hard enough to take off the end of his little finger.

This made him howl and bleed quite a lot until they reached the home of the elf. At that time, the old man made a bandage that stopped the bleeding and spat on the bandage which must have had some good effect for the finger grew back whole and healthy. However, in the meantime, it hurt quite a bit.

The elf's workshop was very disorganized, for he often switched from making one object to the next. No doubt, this was a reason that he completed so few of his projects. Yet he appeared to have what his captors wanted, for he went right to a corner of his shop where he grabbed a spear leaning against the wall.

"It is true, father, that I made this for you long ago, but it is such a wondrous spear I could not part with it. It is made of gold, yet light and strong, nor will it ever miss a target. Throw it at the enemy, and it will never miss. After it has done its deadly work, it will always return to your hand. The name of this spear is *Gungnir*. Once you use it, you will understand why I was loath to give it away."

The spear was so marvelous that the cheating elf was readily forgiven for failing to deliver this magical weapon, for it exceeded all expectations. He did require the elf, though, to give Einar a bag of silver coins for his trouble. By this time, Einar had figured out that his traveling companion was none other than the chief of the Gods. But this gave him no cheer, for he had been scalded by burning soap, had his ankle bitten by a dog, and been knocked into a rocky creek bed and munched on by a mother turtle. The old man invited the youth to accompany him on more adventures, but Einar declined, saying that he had suffered enough and must go to claim his family's inheritance. Thus ended the tale of Einar Evenson and the wondrous Spear of Odin.

Chapter Four

The Tale of the Two Magicians

A contest for a maiden's hand goes awry

"There were in days of old two magicians who lived on the southern tip of Scandia. One was styled as the Red Wizard because his family had painted their farm buildings red for generations. The other magician was called the Blue Wizard because the sail of his ship was dyed a bright blue. Both of them fell in love with the same beautiful woman. It is said that her skin was as white as the snow seen on the tops of distant mountains and her eyes were as blue as the fjord on a clear day. Both of the men courted her with equal ardor, and both of them made equal appeals to her father with gifts of great value. Finally, her father bid her to choose between them as this rivalry of suitors must be ended so that she could be married. But try as she might, she failed to select one over the other. At length, she called them together and said: "I cannot decide which of ye is the better; therefore, this must be decided by the Gods. But as you are not warriors but instead are wizards, the fight must be done by magical methods. You must fight until one of you yields or is slain. Come tomorrow to the meadow next to my father's house. There you will battle for my hand." The two men agreed and retired to their respective homes to prepare for the morrow.

It was then arranged that when the men met the following day that each, in turn, should strike a magical blow as did the heroes of olden days. The Red Wizard, being slightly the elder, was obliged by custom to give the first blow. This he did by summoning an enormous axe in the sky held by a giant hand reaching down from the clouds. The Blue Wizard simply made the clouds into a giant pillow that took the mighty blow of the axe without damage.

The Blue Wizard then called in a pack of ferocious wolves that snapped and yammered in an insane cacophony so loud that it made the bystanders cover their ears. They came out of the woods running full tilt at the wizard; indeed, it looked like he was about to be torn to pieces by the snarling animals. But at the last moment, he transformed them into a flock of small finches that fluttered away harmlessly. Now that the preliminary blows had been given, the two men circled each other warily, trying to figure out the best way of achieving their ends.

The Red Wizard then made some complicated gestures in the air while yelling out some strange incantations. Then he stood with his arms crossed and waited. For a long moment, nothing happened. The Blue Wizard searched the air and the open meadow surrounding them, finding nothing. Then he felt a tremor, in an instant, he shot up into the air, followed close behind by a giant vole that had jumped out of the ground. Only bare inches kept him from falling into its open mouth. When they landed, the wizard sent a spark biting the hindquarters of the beast, which caused it to run off into the neighboring field where it terrorized a village for a week, but as enraged as the villagers became, it's not a part of this story so we'll talk no more about it.

This raised the ire of the Blue Wizard, whose face fairly steamed with anger. He retaliated by sending a Griffin at him. This is a fabulous and dangerous creature with the body of a lion, a head and wings of an eagle, and the tail of a snake. This beast flew around the wizard just out of range of the lightning bolts he threw. He hoped to be able to drain the magic of the Red Wizard by repeatedly darting in at him and then turning aside at the last moment. This went on for quite a while; then the Griffin, seeing the mage weaken, made his attack. The wizard was, just in the nick of time, able to turn the beast into a giant ball of unspun wool at the last minute. He saved his life yet got a painful wound on his shoulder, which caused him to lose his temper entirely.

The Red Wizard then, without thought, cast his most potent curse, one that made him entirely invisible. It was his intention to become invisible so that he could simply walk up to the other wizard and stick his dagger into the man's heart. The spell, although difficult to cast, was successfully made so he actually became invisible. But to his chagrin, it made his body invisible to his own eyes as well, so that he could not see his own feet or hands. This made it more difficult to do simple things like walking. Yet he was determined to have the blood of his rival.

He ran across the meadow as fast as his weakened condition would allow. He felt drained of power from his magical exertions and the loss of blood from his shoulder wound that kept bleeding. As he ran, he, unfortunately, caught his foot in a rabbit hole and fell, hitting his head on a rock so hard it knocked him out.

This confounded the Blue Wizard, who saw his rival disappear without a trace. He waited several hours in vain for the attack. He could only surmise that his rival had been worsted and fled the field of magical battle. He, therefore, took his prize off with him that night. They went to a distant part of Swede Land, from what is said, they prospered mightily.

Things were very different for the Red Wizard, however. He awoke in the night covered in dew in a meadow. He knew it was a meadow, for when he woke, he was trampled by a couple of sheep. They didn't see him, of course, so they just walked on him. This problem of not being seen and therefore not avoided would dog him for some time. He tried to remember the rest of the spell so that he could be restored to his visible self, but the blow on his head had addled his wits.

The next day as he walked unhappily through a village, he was nearly run over by a horse cart that didn't see him. He constantly had to avoid others so that even walking down a village street was fraught with danger. A couple of times he was too slow to act, which caused him to get knocked down. People were always surprised to bump against something that appeared to be nothing.

Eventually, he returned to his abode, where he found a crone, his former nanny, who he acquainted with his predicament. There he lived in seclusion with her, she cared for his needs by going to the market and fending off inquiring neighbors. His only exercise was to walk every day in the woods at the far end of his property.

One day while walking in these woods listening to the sounds of the birds, which were about his only companions in this time of solitude, he saw a man approach. Not just any man, but judging from his size, weapons, and demeanor, this was a berserker. As everyone knows, these are violent men who are undependable in both battle and ordinary life. Those who go into battle with a berserker standing next to them run a double risk, for the berserker is as likely to kill him as the enemy.

This berserker was covered in the skins of wolves and carried many weapons besides the huge club on his shoulder. He wore strands of colored beads, amulets, and trinkets for adornment and was covered with ink marks in the shape of runes. The wizard who could read the runes was deeply shocked, for they were blasphemous texts that invited both Thor and Odin to put their lips to his sexual organ as well as his buttocks. This infuriated the wizard, who was a man careful to respect the Gods. As the man approached, the wizard climbed into a tree in order not to be stepped on by this insane warrior. To his horror, the man stopped and sat under the tree he was sitting in.

From his belt, he took a flask and uncorked it; no doubt this was a herbal concoction used by berserkers and other wild men to soothe their senses and give them dreams. For a long while, he sat at the bottom of the tree in a stupor. The wizard was trapped in the tree, for if he descended invisibly, this wild man would have him. Nor did he have faith in casting a spell on a man like this, for berserkers had a well-known resistance to magical charms. So, there was nothing for it but to sit in an uncomfortable branch and wait.

At length, the man began to stir, although his actions showed him to be still in a befuddled state. From a leather pouch on his belt, he took out several carved wooden idols. He placed one of them in front of him on the ground. He glared at it before saying in a loud voice, "So you think, Sif, that because your hair was returned to your head after Loki stole it makes you a beautiful woman? I scorn you as a low-born chambermaid who is the daughter of slaves. I have considered your case for a long time; I sentence you to execution." Having said this, he took his war club and smote the idol so hard it broke into splinters. This, of course, horrified the devout man sitting above him on the branch. The berserker took another idol, this one God Thor. Regarding it with a sneer on his face, he said, "So this is the great God of Thunder? I scorn you too. You are a fool to let Loki deceive you time after time. Your antics and prating bring no honor at all to Asgard. You can be no true son of the Gods; some dog of a human fathered you. I condemn you to die!" With this, he took his club and hit the small idol so hard that the head came off while the rest was driven into the earth. Of course, the wizard could scarcely maintain his silence as seeing such disgraceful behavior. Yet more was to follow, for he brought forth yet another idol and put it before him. "Father Odin, you pretend to be wise, yet you have allowed the trickster God to make an ass out of you any number of times. Have you no shame? Loki cuckolded you! You drank from the pool of wisdom, yet you have shown no more intelligence than the village idiot. What do you say about these charges? Speak now, or I will end your miserable reign as chief of Asgard. What? You are silent, then feel my righteous wrath as I destroy you!" But as he raised his club to hit the idol, a voice thundered at him from above.

"Hold hard, you brute and blockhead. Not satisfied with the killing of the virtuous Goddess Siff and her husband Thor, you now wish to kill the All-Father himself! Be gone, you vile dog, or I will fry your liver with bolts of lightning!" The berserker looking up to where the voice came from and seeing nothing was so overwhelmed that his face turned blue, and he died on the spot. This amazed the wizard, who dismounted from his perch in the tree. As he stood there regarding the body of the dead berserker, an old man in a grey cloak and wearing a wide-brimmed hat walked into view. He apparently had no trouble seeing him for he walked up to the wizard, looked him in the face, and spoke to him kindly.

"You should check the man's purse; no doubt he has gold that he has stolen from others, for he was a robber besides a berserker. Next time you go to bathe, my friend, use this to wash with." Here he produced a piece of soap that he spit on. He handed it to the astonished wizard and bid him farewell as he walked through the wood. The wizard followed the old man's advice, for he knew that he had talked to the Spear-Shaker himself. Indeed, the berserker had many gold coins hidden inside his belt. As for using the soap, he found that it removed the cover of invisibility so that he returned to his natural self. He was then able to take up his former life, where he eventually married a woman who bore him a number of children in complete happiness.

Chapter Five

The Man of No Fate

Odin Confounds the Norns

The wise have likened magic to a great stream that flows like a river under the earth. It runs northward, crisp, and clear, through the old land of the Saxons toward the misty Sea of Frisia. From thence, it branches to the east, where it flows under the land of the Finns. But the Finns, it's said, were, of all people, the ones least suited to the use of magic. They are silent and brooding folk given to dark moods. Nonetheless, they are often accused of being able to call forth storms which makes them unpopular with sailors. But savants maintain that this is naught but a filthy lie; there might be reasons to dislike the Finns but not on this account.

In Scandia, magic blossomed and bloomed, adding song and beauty to the world. Certain families had, it's said, *dangled their toes in the magical river.* It is from such a magical family that the first master of runes sprang from long ago among those who dwelt in the wild country north of the Swedes; his name is not known yet he was the first to perceive the link between the runes which Odin hung on the tree for, and inborn magical ability. For when magic is mixed with runes by a savant, enormous power is possible.

It should not be said that all those who use magic do so out of a kind nature any more than all of them keep oaths. Some who have this gift are too insane to use it. Others, the kind most dangerous, are insane but have the will and ability to act normal yet cast spells that bring ruin to everyone unfortunate enough to be close to them. Among the writings of Gunnar, the Bald, a mighty and wise Runemaster, was found a curious reference as to how Father Odin was able to circumvent the limitations of inborn human power set for every person upon their birth. For the fates decreed that no person could do other than submit to the future ordained for them, and this included the use of runes that were too powerful for mortals to play with. Even the Chief of the Gods had to suffer a gruesome torment to gain their use. But they reckoned without the fertile mind of the One-Eyed Dreamer; here follows the means by which he set fate aside.

"It is known to the wise that our fate is set by the damsels known as the Nornim, who sit at the roots of Yggdrasil, the great Tree of Life. Surrounding the roots is the great pool of Living Waters where all knowledge can be found. It was there that father Odin gave one of his eyes for a single cup of the knowing water from this wondrous fountain. Upon sticks of wood, the Nornim carve our fates on the day of our birth.

"One day, long ago, the witch maiden Skuld took a length of wood to carve the fate of a newborn boy upon. Yet when she tried to cut the wood, it proved refractory; try as she might, she could make no mark.

"'Sisters, I cannot make a mark upon this bough. This is exceedingly strange.'"

"'Your blade has become dull; hie it to the dwarfs to get it sharpened,'" said the Norn Verdandi.

"This was done by the carver of fate, yet when she resumed her seat in the shade of the mighty Tree of Life, she found that her blade could still make no mark upon the wood. Angered, she flung the piece far away, thinking it was somehow defective; it sailed far into the distance. "'Let the wolves chew on it if they can; maybe this child's future will be the tooth marks of an animal, or maybe no fate at all.'" At this, she and her sisters laughed at the thought of a man with no fate. Then they turned aside to other work forgetting all about this matter.

The Norns of Fate who sit under Yggdrasil, the Tree of Life

"Yet not long after this errant branch of empty destiny landed upon the ground, an old beggar, dressed in a long grey cloak and wide-brimmed hat of the same color, walked by, and deftly grabbed the piece of wood and hid it under his robes. A short time later, he approached the stream that ran out of Asgard carrying the excess magical waters from the Well of Life that bathed the roots of the Tree of Life; once these magical waters left the home of the Gods, they flowed to Midguard, the world in which we mortals dwell in; once here it streamed like a river under the lands we live in and giving mortals a great magical power; at least to those who learned how to find and control it.

"The old man stopped at the stream's edge, where he uttered a long spell before spitting upon the wood. Then gently placed it into the bubbling stream and watched it as it floated away. After the piece of wood had gone out of sight on its way to the world of men, he gave a hearty chuckle at once more being able to exercise his own will upon creation.

"Thus did the All-Father, the Delight of Frigg, the One-Eyed Dreamer, give a man a destiny that was his own to make without the lashings and sleet of fate beating down upon his brow. This man, whose name is hidden, was the first to entwine the magic that flowed out of Asgard with the runes of Odin. It was he who discovered the sun-hidden, stone-strong rules of rune mastery. It was he who guarded the dead with runes placed on stones above them after they died and worked so many other mighty feats of magic. All the Runemasters who followed owe their abilities to this one man, a man with no fate."

-Translated from the original Latin documents containing the *Saga of Merila Argisdottar* by John Borough of Sandwich, Garter King of Arms, November 1636.

Chapter Six

The Tale of Heimdall's Shoes

The God of the Gate Gives Loki the Boot

In the days of old, when the dwarfs were friendlier with the Gods and men, the dwarf Brokor was visiting Asgard when he noticed that the God Heimdall was walking as if his feet hurt him.

"What ails thee that thou can't walk in a normal fashion?"

"My shoes are worn out, master dwarf. I tread these walls daily, as is my task. Alas, leather lasts but a short time because of my constant pacing."

"I will fix that in a trice," replied the dwarf, "let me see your feet so that I might gauge their size." This the dwarf did after the God had removed his shoes which were on the verge of falling apart. The dwarf then went to his workshop, where that night, he made a pair of shoes for his friend Heimdall. He used the leather of seals that is well-suited for fine shoes. He also cast such spells on them that only dwarf shoemakers know. The next day he took them to the God's post upon the walls of Asgard.

"Here, my friend, are shoes fit for a God. They will never wear out, nor will your feet become tired while wearing them. Not only will your feet rejoice at never feeling tired or pinched, the shoes will lend your feet great strength. If a door ever is locked against thee, a single kick from you will break it into pieces."

This pleased Heimdall so greatly that he gave the dwarf so much gold that he could scarcely carry it.

"This not a fair recompense that thou hast given me," said the dwarf, "too much you have rewarded me. So, I leave you the flute I made for the old king of Courland, who died before I could give it to him. It is magical, of course, for no matter how unskilled the musician plays, the sound will always be melodious." Heimdall took the gift with great appreciation, although he never played it. He had little taste for music because his duties on the wall required him to always use his hearing. Indeed, it was on Heimdall that the Gods depended on to keep watch over the malevolent lands beyond Asgard's broad plains. For there lived monsters. Sometimes they would find a way to avoid the many spells that confined them to their world. Forever they strove to invade the realm of men where they could enjoy an unholy slaughter of humans. If any broke free, Heimdall would know it. He could hear the sound of wool growing on the back of sheep; he could even hear a single leaf falling in a forest. But if any foul creature escaped, he would report it to Thor, who would go forth in his chariot to fight the invaders. It was also Heimdall's duty to listen for the sounds of the great ravaging army coming on the final day to fight the Last Battle with the Gods for the supremacy of the nine worlds.

One winter's night, when the sounds of men accounted but little as they were all sleeping in their cottages, a sound was heard by Heimdall coming from a home on top of a hill in Hunland. A man who dwelled there took it upon himself to play the flute. The sound he made was so vile and wretched that it would have scared away the very horses of the Valkyrie, who were used to the terrible sounds of battle and death. Luckily none were in the area. The noise drifted over the hills, which alarmed the trolls so much that they hid in their hovels with their hands over their ears. For poor Heimdall, it was nothing but a torment to hear this unskilled musician at his work. This continued for several days until the great God of the Gate was nigh flummoxed about what to do. Just as he was about to summon Thor to deal with this false musician, he saw

Loki walking by. This gave Heimdall an idea; he recalled the magic flute given to him by the dwarf. He knew too, that Loki was indebted to him for several things he had done for him; he asked Loki to take this flute to the man in Hunland to replace the rebellious instrument that robbed him of his peace. Loki could do naught else, for he was under deep obligations to Heimdall. So, when Heimdall gave him a sack that contained the flute, he promised to give the bag to the man in Hunland.

But Loki, being of an untrustworthy nature, tried to think of ways that he could keep the instrument for himself. He played it as he walked along, well pleased by its sound.

While walking in Hunland, he saw a dead stallion that had recently died lying next to the path. This gave him an idea, for he had promised to give the sack to the man, but no mention was made of what was inside it. After a brief stop, he was on his way again. Later that same day, he spied the farm of the one whom he was seeking on top of a hill. With a smile, Loki walked up to the house, where he found the farmer sharpening a scythe.

"Greetings, my friend," said Loki as he walked up to the farm, "the music you play at night has been heard as far away as Asgard. The God Heimdall, who tends the gate, wishes to reward you and your skill by giving you this fine instrument that he wishes you to put to your lips tonight. He says that once your mouth has touched it, the music that comes out will be unlike anything you have played thus far." After handing the sack to the bewildered farmer, he turned on his heel and made off. The farmer, after seeing this strange behavior emptied the contents of the bag on the grass in front of him, revealing the large phallus of a horse.

As Loki left to retrieve that magical flute from where he had hidden it, the farmer stamped his foot and cried out, "What manner of God wishes to make a fool of an honest farmer by giving him the cock of a horse to play on? *This* is what he wants me to wrap my lips around? What sort of sound does he think *that* would make? May the hammer pound his skull a hundred times!" The farmer reviled the unwitting God of the

Gate with these curses and many others. Needless to say, the music at night did not improve.

At length, Heimdall called upon the dwarf Fili to help him discover what went wrong. Fili could turn himself into a bird which was very useful for spying on people. He found Loki a few days later, walking towards Asgard playing a fine-sounding flute. When he reported this to Heimdall the God knew immediately that the dishonest Loki had once again betrayed the trust of another. He then resolved to pay Loki back. He gave a message to the dwarf to take to Loki, saying that he had a special prize that he wanted to give him for carrying out his errand to Hunland so successfully. Loki, when he heard this, wondered what had happened. Perhaps, he thought, the farmer had given up his attempts at music. In that case, Heimdall would be grateful to him.

When Loki came to Asgard, Heimdall greeted him with friendly words. He told him that he had a special reward for him. Loki saw that many people had gathered around, so he began to suspect that it was a great gift indeed that he would get. Heimdall called Loki over to where he stood with people gathered behind him.

"Loki, you have earned your fee for taking that sack to the farmer whose music needed improving. Many days have I thought about how to repay you; now, I have found a gift worthy of your deeds." Here Heimdall put his arm around Loki as the crowd cheered. "I put it under that small pot just over there." said the God pointing to a brass bowl a few feet away, "if you will be good enough to lift it, you can bring the great prize underneath it over here so that all can see."

Loki did as he was told; he walked forward a few paces to where the kettle was placed and bent over to retrieve it.

At this point, Loki was given his reward sooner than he had imagined for Heimdall, wearing the magical shoes which gave immense power to his feet and legs, booted Loki so hard on his buttocks that he flew over the wall a hundred paces away. The sound that Loki made when he went sailing through the air was considered to be the loudest musical event ever heard in Asgard. At this, everyone cheered at the discomfiture of Loki, for all knew how richly he deserved such treatment!

Loki Gets His Reward

Chapter Seven

How the King Got His Magical Talisman

A Norse King Finds Friendship Rewarded

In my studies, I found a curious bit of lore about an enchanted diadem that saved the life of a great king whose might and sagacity have come down to us from the ages. This story was recorded by an anonymous churchman and historian in the *Regibus Danorum*.

"It was in the time of King Bjorn Bjornson the Old that the Danes began to take on a more national character; this was continued under his son, the Great King Baldur Bjornson. For he put down the numerous petty kings who ruled various islands and coastal areas whose main pastime was fighting with each other to the detriment of their people. Bjornson was a man of superior intelligence and ability besides having a constitution like an ox and strength to match. He was also a renowned swimmer and wrestler, which impressed the people greatly. However, in some old tales, he is called *King Short-Beard Bjornson* or even *King Bjornson the Red-Nosed*. He was given those appellations due to the coins he had made and what became of them.

When Bjorn Bjornson came to the high throne, it was considered proper that coins be struck in his realm as in other kingdoms; it was done, but the result was poor for the skill of the Danes in coinage had yet to be uncovered, and this effort was but pitiful. The King called in a Greek master who had made coins for various kings and rulers of their largest realms and cities. He made splendid coins with the picture of the King on one side and a likeness of the All-Father's ravens on the other. This pleased the King to no end, yet when cheating churls took to clipping the coins to gain silver by such means, the King's beard often became short. Worse yet, some of the counterfeiters made coins out of base metal with only a thin wash of silver over them; when the silver wore off, the King's nose on the coin came off first, giving him the visage of a red-nosed sot. This infuriated the King, who then held a court of assizes to inquire into why his beautiful coins were being defaced. This was held in Lindholm in Jutland at the annual meeting.

The Jarls sent him several men who were caught clipping coins. Since these men clipped coins, the King declared that they should help build the famous ship Nagelfar, mentioned in sagas as being made entirely from the clippings of dead men's fingers and toenails. With that in mind, he had the ends of their fingers and toes cut off as offerings to the Gods. As for the red nose of the coin caused by inferior metals, he had the two men responsible brought before him so that he could punch each one in the nose; their noses were very red indeed by the time the King got done with them. The populace took these actions as proof of the King's high regard for justice and his great sagacity. Indeed, there was much support in the land for the King's new laws.

The greatest evil in the land was, in those times, the practice of the strong landowners taking the lands of their weaker neighbors. Very often, it was done without even a crumb of justification. The land was the most valuable thing in the Norse countries, for much of it is infertile sandy soil or barren rock. Good farmland was so coveted that men stayed up late into the night plotting how to get more of it. Another evil was depriving people of their inheritance; many a firstborn son had his parent's farm taken away, forcing him to spend his days as a simple farm worker. Therefore, the King passed laws regarding the ownership of land. This made him popular among the people, except for the wealthy landowners who resented his interference. At the annual folkmoot, called *The Thing*, several men were outlawed the following year for taking land that wasn't theirs; this caused hard feelings among some landowners. One of those who despised the King for his new laws was Lard Ringson, a greedy and wealthy Dane who had stolen by various underhanded means land in every district of the kingdom; he also attempted to take the kingdom for himself when Bjorn the Old struggled to establish his rule. Like all of those who backed the wrong horse in the contest, he lost heavily. He wished, above all else, to harm the King, but he was a coward who would not face him directly, so he employed craft and guile to oppose him. Despite what the sagas say, there are always more cowardly men than brave ones.

In the third year of Bjornson's rule, Jarl Lard Ringson perpetrated a filthy trick upon the King, making the ruler the butt of many jokes. Word spread that the King was marrying his niece to Prince Hortini of the Geats. This was considered a good match for her because he was handsome, well-mannered, and rich. The King's niece, Helga, was famed for her beauty and virtue; of course, she would bring both land and coin into the marriage. The youth was something of a dandy, for his warship had a sail with their household emblem of a seal on it, for they had made much money in hunting seals; their coats are sought because they are both warm and resist water. In the spring, they awaited the prince's arrival, so lookouts were posted at the entry to the fiord; when the signal was given, everyone would go to the docks to greet this important youth.

The ship was seen approaching the docks, but those with sharp eyes saw things they couldn't account for. For one thing, the emblem on the sail appeared to be the wrong shape to be a seal; in fact, it looked much more like a pig's face. There was something odd, too, about the men of the ship with their brightly colored shirts and coats. They appeared to run around on the deck in a most unseemly manner. But when the ship failed to furl its sail and run out its oars, everyone knew something was wrong. The ship missed the dock entirely, sailing right past it only to crash into the shoreline some distance up the fjord. But as it went by, the astonished watchers could see that there was no crew aboard, only pigs and goats who wore, as best as they could, old shirts and trousers that were held on with twine. And the emblem on the sail was indeed a pig. The maid was sent swine and goats that day instead of a husband! As the men looked from the dock, they could see another ship picking up a rowboat; it was obvious that whoever had perpetrated this hoax had tied the tiller in place and then left, utilizing a small boat that was now being picked up by the larger vessel. It was impossible to see who it was at this distance, but later the King made inquiries that revealed to him who had perpetrated the ruse. His niece, being of a practical mind, had the animals taken to her farm and gave a hearty laugh at the whole episode. Such was her self-confidence that she could take pleasure even in something that attempted to cast her in a bad light. The prince, when he arrived, said little but in his private prayers to Thor; he expressed a wish to meet in battle those who had done this; later, his wish was granted.

Many Kings would have taken Lard Ringson and roasted him slowly over a fire, but Lard calculated that King Bjornson was too weak to do that. Indeed, the King didn't retaliate immediately because he knew that the cost to others was more than he was willing to pay; any time there is a quarrel between the powerful, it's the small people who pay most of the butcher's bill. This, of course, weakens the kingdom, besides causing great suffering. Indeed, sometimes the warfare is so intense that there is nobody left to harvest the crops, and great areas of land go fallow while the people starve. This benevolent attitude, uncommon among rulers, was adhered to by his son Baldur whose rule was later held forth by historians as the model for the way rulers should act.

The King did strike back at Lard Ringson the following year when the Jarl was accused at the annual Thing of stealing horses. Indeed, this man was a notorious horse thief, but he had grown careless over the years. The people, except for his underlings and those who fear him, who were many, had enough of his ways. He was accused by four people of theft. At first, the Jarl demanded trial by combat, intending to hire a berserker to fight in his stead when the King ruled that all such contests must be done in person without a substitute. He further stated that the person representing the poor people, who had no arms or ability to fight, would be none other than himself. The idea of going up against the King, who was a renowned warrior, put such fear in his bowels as to cause him to accept a sentence of five years as an outlaw, which was the maximum penalty that could be imposed on him. As it was, the people got little relief from that Jarl's predatory efforts because when he left for exile, he took several ships and their crews and went raiding. He destroyed farms and small villages while always evading the forces that the various kings sent against him. In doing so, he became very rich in plunder and slaves. Yet being made an outlaw rankled him to the point that he couldn't sleep at night; he decided to kill the King, for he knew that Bjornson, by this time, was resolved to have his blood without fail.

The Talisman of Protection

The Jarl met a bard in one of the larger cities of Flanders who always needed money due to excessive spending on drinking, gambling, and whores. He agreed to pay him a large amount of gold if he would go to the court of King Bjornson and poison him. At first, the man was unwilling to do so, but the Jarl explained that the poison was slow to work, often taking days to kill a man. This would allow him plenty of time to get away and return to Ghent, where he would be paid his due. The bard had a good voice and spoke the Balt trade language well. However, the Jarl also taught him some songs that were then popular among the Danes to assure him of a good audience. For days they practiced together, the man being diligent in his quest to learn these songs and earning the ten marks of gold that was promised him. He was mistaken in this since the jarl lied about the poison. The King would have died a horrible death within just a few moments of taking the potion; his dreams of wealth and riotous living was doomed from the start.

As it turned out, the King's life was spared because the bard was recognized by a slave who was a captured man of Flanders. He told the King that the bard was a known thief who couldn't be trusted with anything, including the wives of other men. The King had the man seized and questioned in a very harsh manner; he revealed the plot entirely, and as a punishment, the contents of the bottle that was found in his possession were poured down his throat, causing him to perish miserably. Of course, the slave was given his freedom and made rich. The King then declared the life of the Jarl to be forfeit and that anyone who killed him would earn his favor. This made the Jarl frantic to kill the King before this sentence could be carried out. But as the King was now too well guarded to try another assassination, he had to bide his time, so he took his ships a-roving, harrying the coast of the Franks and Less Britain. Yet he was always thinking of ways to take the King's life. Nor was he alone, for he had numerous relatives who could profit from the death of King Bjornson. One of these was Gunnwalder Varison, who was a low outlaw and raider who lived carefully hidden away in some wild and remote islands in the north of the Sweden coast. He had offended so many jarls with his thievery and errant cruelty that he was forced to live in constant fear for his life.

It came to pass that this criminal, by chance, found out that the King was going to spend yule with King of the Geats at his estate that was at least twenty miles from the sea, and to get there, he would have to travel up the frozen river to get to the King's home. This seemed to him to be a golden opportunity to waylay King Bjornson and kill him; doubtless, he would get a huge reward from his kinsman Lard Ringson. To this end, they took their ships to the mouth of the river and searched for a suitable spot to ambush the King, who was due to arrive any day. To assist in their plot, they brought a dozen sturdy horses shod for ice. They planned to hide along the bank, and when they spotted his sleigh coming up the river, they would charge out from behind the trees and bushes and kill him with their long spears. The major shortcoming of this plan was that they were forced to camp in the wilds, where the snow blew, and the wolves howled.

Afterward, men would talk of the wonderful craft and guile of the plan, which certainly would have worked if the ice had been thicker. When Gunnwalder and his men charged out in hot pursuit of the two-horse sleigh, it was a very near thing as the King was almost alone; he had only a couple of retainers with him then. Indeed, they were within a hundred feet of him when they hit a weak spot in the ice, and Gunnwalder and his men disappeared from view until the thaw next spring when their bodies were found downriver on a sandbar. Of course, the King gave an offering to the Gods for sparing his life, yet he wondered how many more attempts he would survive.

At the great feast that King Hrothgar of the Geats held, King Bjornson met a famous man named Eyestein the far traveled, who earned a great reputation for visiting many places, some quite distant. This man spent much time with the King and became good friends. Later that year, after the ice melted, he sailed into the Kattegat and stayed with King Bjornson for many weeks; before he left, he gave the King a diadem with a beautiful central jewel held between two silver dragons that he valued greatly, but he thought that the King's need for it was much greater than his.

"This is more than just a pretty bauble," explained Eyestein, "it might someday save your life. It contains a spell that will warn you whenever someone of ill intent is near you. It will spring to life, and you'll feel it radiate warmth and pulse-like unto a beating heart."

"That would be a wondrous thing if true," replied the King skeptically.

"You can rely on it; once, when I was traveling in the far and distant realm east of the South Rus, I stayed with my men at the home of a nobleman. As we were feasting and merry-making, I felt it grow in warmth and throbbing power. That night while my men slept and snored like a pack of hounds, I stayed awake. Just before the hour of the owl, I heard a noise, and by the feeble light of the fire, I saw one of the nobleman's henchmen approaching with a sword in his hand. But just as he raised the tip to thrust it into me, I sprang up and planted my knife into his belly. Then I clamped my hands around his throat to prevent him from crying out. By then, my men were awake and reaching for their weapons. We left as stealthily as we could from a side door and then made for the gate; by the time the sun rose, we were many miles ahead."

"This is a great tale, but how came you of it?"

"I bought it from a merchant who I saved from certain death while traveling the wildlands near the big lake that men call the Black Sea. He took only a handful of silver for it saying that it was worth much more than that. It had been made in a mountainous region even further to the east where strange Gods hold sway. A priest of a demon cult made this object in an age long past and put his life essence in it. There is not another like it in the whole world, yet you need it more than I do."

So that is how King Bjornson the Old came to have the marvelous circlet that he wore on his brow until his death, after which it came to his son King Baldur Bjornson. Yet before death claimed him in old age, the King was shown the great value of the gift given to him by his boon companion Eyestein the far traveled for one more time did, Jarl Lard Ringson attempt to kill him.

The following Yule King Bjornson was holding court in his large estate. His feasting hall was big enough to hold a hundred people, for he showed hospitality to many people, especially his neighbors.

One day a traveling cobbler showed up offering to repair shoes and boots. This was not unusual for such men often traveled the roads putting on new heels and soles. He repaired a couple of pairs of shoes, but before he left, he offered for sale a small jar of a special ointment made, he said, from the liver of the night vole. This is a mysterious creature notoriously hard to find, but few look for them, though, since they have long, sharp front teeth and are ill-tempered enough to use them if annoyed. But the peddler said that the oil taken from this vole liver was the best in the world for softening leather boots while at the same time waterproofing them. For a price of only a couple of coppers and the promise of a place to sleep that night, he agreed to part with that small bottle of the ointment.

Yet the man was not a peddler; no, he was an assassin in the employ of Jarl Ringson. He had been working as a laborer on a nearby farm, where he kept his mouth shut and ears open, hoping to learn something useful. In time he did learn of something to his advantage, for he found that the King had been given a pair of new boots as a gift from one of his jarls. This gave him the opportunity he had waited for; it's a fact that all new boots are very uncomfortable at first because the leather is so stiff. He was careful to say that she wasn't to rub this oil on using bare hands for it's very strong and might cause the fingertips to burn and crack. The woman took heed of that advice and put it on with a small brush. The peddler left the next day confident that once the King put those boots on that had been treated with that poison, he would soon die.

However, this new plan was doomed to failure, for the King had taken to wearing the circlet that Eyestein had given him every day. For even if it didn't have a magical charm within it, he thought, it was a great feat of craftsmanship. When it came time for him to try on his new boots, he felt a terrible pain on his brow so strong that he was compelled to draw back; this happened several times with the same result. But as it only happened with the boots present, the King grew suspicious of them, so he called for Eyestein and bid him investigate the matter. Upon questioning the household, he learned of this so-called oil made from the liver of the much-maligned night vole. He smelled the contents of the jug and said it was a rank poison made from the flowers found among the Greeks far to the south. It was a common poison in those parts, and all high-highborn persons and travelers had been warned against it. The King put his nose to the jug and smelled it too; its smell was as vile as aged badger dung. Needless to say, no more oils or ointments were ever purchased again from traveling peddlers. And when the time came for Eyestein to return to his home, he was loaded down with many fine gifts.

This most recent assassination attempt infuriated the King, who cast about searching for a way to kill Jarl Ringson, for he knew that with enough attempts, sooner or later, the outlaw Jarl would find a way to slay him. Then Eyestein told him of a family of assassins who were employed sometimes by a nobleman of the Northern Rus who was under an obligation to him for previous favors. The man lived on the shore of Lake Ladoga, which was easy to find as this region did a certain amount of trading with the Norse, especially the Swedes. The king sent a messenger to the nobleman along with Eyestein's ring to show who it was that requested that service as a favor; scarce a month later, a ship returned with a woman who gave Eyestein his ring back with the words that by sending her to him all old debts had been paid. Eyestein took the ring and was content; as for the woman, whose name is not recorded, she listened intently to all that the King and others had to say about Jarl Lard Ringson, then she demanded a ship, not a warship but one that would attract less attention, so she was given an ordinary trading vessel the type that merchants most commonly use.

Nothing was heard of her for a long time until the following year, just as the raiding season started when she returned. Saying but little, she

walked up to the King and handed him a bag; in it was the head of Jarl
Lard Ringson. The King was astonished, for by now, he had pretty much
given up hope that she would accomplish anything. He thought that
perhaps this woman had taken the ship, returned home, and then sold
the vessel making the King the victim of a scheme.

"How did you kill him?" he asked as he sat dumbfounded.

"You know, King Bjornson, that the main weakness of men, as well
as their strength, hangs between their legs. I used this fact to my
advantage. The only real difficulty was in finding out where this man had
hidden. It took much effort and bribes to find that he was not so far
away after all. Long ago, I found that when a man wishes to hide, he will
often go to a relative, if he has one, in a distant place. So, when I found
out that he had a cousin who lived on a tiny island off the coast of the
Geats, I suspected that he might winter there as he was no longer
welcome among the Franks or the Frisians or anywhere else for that
matter because of his murderous rages and parsimony. Those stupid
enough to take service under him did so simply because nobody else
would have them. Yet other fools followed him in hopes of plunder.

"We pretended to be travelers who had trouble with our ship and
needed to make repairs. I claimed to be a recently widowed woman
whose husband had been hung for violating Your Majesty's laws. I
roundly cursed these new laws saying that it was unfair to punish men
for simply following the will of the Gods who teach us that the strong
deserve more than the weak. This recommended me to him, and the
more time we spent together, the greater his desire for me grew. I became
friendly with this miserable lout. I agreed to dally with him in his private
quarters, but I had no intention of giving myself to that swine. I put a
potion in his wine which caused him to sleep soundly, and late that night,
when all was quiet, I took his sword and cut off his head. Then I got my
men, who were waiting for me, snuck out of his quarters, and made our
escape."

The King was only too happy to pay her the marks of gold that he
had promised for the Jarl's life. He ordered his men to take her back

home to the Rus and gave her gifts besides the reward. Ever afterward, he wore the circlet around his head and praised the generosity of his friend Eyestein who gave the charming jewel to him. And in the fullness of time, he gave it to his son Baldur who followed him as King.

Chapter Eight

The Storm Queen

A Sensible Woman Makes a Bargain

In the olden days, there was a wealthy landowner named Bjarn Havardson, known to all as *Bjarn the tall*. This was just after King Dag became the high ruler of the Geats. He had a wife named Britt who gained fame because once, while alone with just her young children with her, a pair of robbers beset her; she killed one of them by sticking him in the throat with a pitchfork; the other man she chased out of the barn after cutting his left ear off with a knife. They had two sons who left as soon as they were strong enough to go raiding, leaving their sister to stay home to care for her parents. Her name was Gertrud, who everyone called *Gertrud the Fair*. Her name meant *spear* in the old language, which was very apt as she was tall and inclined to be rather thin. She was a girl of good common sense who never took on airs over her beauty, rightfully observing that beauty is in the eye of the beholder.

She was a virtuous maiden who would never see a man alone except for an old peddler who showed up at her door selling thread, needles, and scissors. She paid little attention to the man whose rough grey cloak was the same color as his wide-brimmed hat. His lowly station was shown by his worn sandals, besides using a piece of rope for a belt. Yet the scissors impressed her with their blueish tint, and when she used them to cut a piece of thick material, they cut through as quickly as if she were cutting butter. The price for his wares was reasonable, so they soon struck a bargain; she paid him in silver, and after sending him to the kitchen to be fed, she was always conscientious about the rules of hospitality; she and her maids then left to bathe in a nearby stream.

The peddler heard of her plan as he was leaving, showing a spryness that belied his age; he ran to the stream, where he found a good hiding spot to see what he could see. What he saw was a naked beauty that was the fairest he had seen in many moons, and he was in a position to know since he had many famous beauties in his time. He was no ordinary peddler; he was Odin, the All-Father, the Spear-Shaker, and the Enemy of the Wolf. His passion was stirred until his blood boiled within him. He resolved to have her no matter what the cost. Nor could many ever have refused him, for he knew a spell that, when cast, would make any woman tremble with lust at his touch.

Shortly afterward, Gertrud's parents left for a few days to attend a feast in the hall of a jarl; she didn't go because she found the sotted behavior of the man obnoxious. The following afternoon a warrior rode his horse up to the house and dismounted. He was a large man bursting with strength and vitality. There was grey in his hair and beard, yet his manner was that of a man in his prime; he carried with him a long bright spear and wore a silver corselet and a golden helm decorated with eagle wings; on his arms were silver rings and inked designs of the most curious sort.

Being an intelligent girl, she knew that this was Odin, the All-Father and the One-Eyed Dreamer. He wore a patch over his missing right eye, the one he gave up in his quest for knowledge at the Pool of Knowledge that flowed under Yggdrasil, the tree of life. She immediately recognized him, although he had previously taken the disguise of an old peddler, a man with both eyes; yet now she saw him in his true form.

It thrilled her to behold the chief of the Gods, yet it filled her with apprehension because of his reputation of sporting with beautiful women; it was said that few could evade his charms. As he tied his steed to the tree branch, her maiden's mind was filled with wild thoughts. Would she be able to resist his advances? And did she even *want* to resist them? Being, above all things, a bright and practical girl, she resolved to hear what he had to say before letting her emotions rule her; if a God insisted on having her, there was little that she could do to prevent it; yet if she dallied with him on terms, she might be rewarded.

She continued sitting in her chair under a vast spreading oak tree, doing her needlework as he approached; she pretended not to see him, yet she had a clear view of him as he drew near. He paused a few steps before her and mumbled some words into his beard while making passes with his hands in the air in front of him. He waited expectantly but what he waited for wasn't clear; then he repeated his actions with the same result; when he attempted it a third time, she couldn't contain herself any longer and laughed aloud, asking him why he was so intent on shooing away horseflies.

"Nay, 'tis not the horseflies that I drive away," laughed the God, "but you have driven away my strongest suit to woo you with. Know ye that you are filled with magic? No? Yet it is sooth, fair maid."

"Would that I had magic, Father, for I would have used it to calm the tempest that sank two of our fishing boats just a month ago, leaving mothers weeping for their sons. The common folk have so little that it seems cruel to rob them of their sons, the only candles they have to shed light unto their lives."

"You have the power within your, fair Gertrud; you lack only the knowledge to use it. There has not been a weather witch in the world for quite some time to tame the storms and master the winds. Are you woman enough to call forth the wild magic from your soul and the earth? Are you so bold?"

"I have ever been bold, which is why suitors come not to my door. The young men look at me like I am an untamed horse. But you will want a night of sport with me, one that no doubt will put me with child. A woman with a child and no husband is considered churlish and wanton."

"It is ever so young maid that the bellies of those I have lain with have produced children, yet I would not disgrace you. I have a young blade in mind; he is a Prince of the Goths, and his father owes me much. Lay with me tonight, and I will send him to you, for he is a strong lad who will not quail at the words of a willful woman. He has proved himself in battle often, yet it is not strife and the blows of axes he wants; he desires to plant and reap the good things of the earth. He is a true man whose farm will be the envy of all. Strike a bargain with me now, and I will teach you the weirding ways of the weather and give you a fine husband. What say you?" To this, she smiled and agreed; he then stood next to her, whispered spells into her ears, and gave her the knowledge of the weather-wise. With a bit of practice, she could summon clouds like Mother Freya; she learned how to talk to the wind to make it her servant. Like unto the spinning of wool in her mind, she would gather the dark clouds and squeeze them of their water. In time she became the secret savant of the seasons and the power of her magic. This she passed on to her daughter and from these to the following generations, always female because the Norns of fate who sit by the Pool of Knowledge ordained it so.

The Storm Queen

Her life was one of joy for her, and her husband was a perfect match. He was honest, high-born, and had eyes only for his wife. They had many children, but the firstborn, a girl, was, in turn, known as a great beauty, just like her mother.

Yet in the quiet of a winter's night when she sat late in front of the fire sipping wine, she recalled the night she did sport with the Chief of the Gods. Her first night of pleasure with a man that was a God made her smile in memory. It was her secret joy that she shared with none other.

When the time came that her years were fulfilled and she lay in the coffin to the sobs of her children and grandchildren, there came a warrior to the house who brought a wreath of flowers that he laid at her feet. Then taking a teardrop from his eye, he put it on her lips with his finger. This done, the one-eyed man left, leaving all in wonder at who he was and whence he came. So ended the life of the first of the line of weather-witches of the north who did so much to save the people's lives.

Chapter Nine

The Twilight of the Gods

The Tale of the End Times According to the Northmen: Ragnarok, the Last Battle

It is appointed unto all things to die. All men and all creatures perish, as the earth that we stand on will one day come to an end. Even the mighty tree of life and eternity that holds up the worlds of existence will one day become only so much firewood. This cannot be helped as it is the natural order. When one world dies in old age, another will be reborn if allowed to, yet there are fell creatures who would prevent this rebirth if they could.

To them, all life, even their own, is hateful, so they wish to destroy all things. They want to kill the Gods of Asgard and all living things here in Midguard, the place that is called *middle-earth*. What do these creatures look like? Much talk is devoted to that subject, but all that is known is that there will be wolves of monstrous size, birds that fly who have heads of boars, brute trolls with hides thicker than the best armor, two-headed bears, dragons who spit fire, bats the size of horses and turtles with sharp and strong jaws with shells so big that they could easily be used as a house. As we sit here today, these fell beings are of no account to us, for they are kept in place by powerful magical spells. When a few of them escape, that happens now and again; Thor will track them down and beat them with his hammer.

Yet there will come a time when the magic containing these creatures will weaken and fail. There will be some warning signs, though. One will be that we will have three unnaturally long winters in a row that will bring about much famine followed closely by diseases; many will perish, others will be lost as they try to sail to warmer seas south of us; others will go to Frankia or travel to the sea of no tides. The moon's cycles will change as it comes haphazardly to the sky at night, nor will the days be normal length. All this shall drive some men mad as they kill their own families before skulking off into the woods to live like wild beasts in caves and dens.

The priests will offer sacrifices to the Gods, yet the Gods cannot provide any relief from the suffering. Besides madmen, there will be criminals who will cast off all restraint roaming the countryside and villages, killing, and raping wherever they can. Oath-breaking and incest shall be seen everywhere as the world of man descends into chaos. Eventually, the moon will hide in clouds for shame over what mortals do.

Frigg, Wife of Odin and Warriors on The Last Day

Then will come a day that the God Heimdall, the Keeper of the Gate at Asgard, shall hear sounds that will send him hurrying to blow

Gallerhorn, the mighty horn of doom that will be heard all over the nine worlds. For he has heard, many leagues away, the sound of the monster hoard breaking free from the wards that kept them fenced within their lands. Now that the warning has sounded, the Gods and the worthy dead will rouse themselves to fight for the world to be reborn. It is a simple matter, really; if the Gods defeat the hideous creatures on the Plains of Vigrid, then life will be renewed so that a new race of men will arise to till the fields and hunt in the forests. But if we are defeated, then darkness will evermore overwhelm all life. The land will die cold and barren. This time, called *Ragnarok,* will see the last battle fought on the last day of our world.

Father Odin will come striding out of his palace as the dwarfs readied his armor and brought forth his steed, the mighty Sleipnir, a fabulous horse of eight legs. He shall carry the famed spear Gungnir that never misses its target. After he throws it, the spear always returns to his hand. The All-Father will wear a helmet of gold with armor made of bright silver, all wondrously wrought by the dwarfs. As Odin waits for his forces to be marshaled behind him, the God Braggi, now in bronze armor, brings forth his harp from out of his house. While the troops assemble, he sings songs of war with his melodious voice. His wife Idune, now in a tunic of silver ring mail, makes one more trip to the garden of immortality, where she makes a final harvest of the fruit that gives life-renewing strength to the Gods. As the Gods leave Asgard for the plains of battle, she will give them one last apple from her basket. Among Odin's large family, the God Thor is the mightiest; his magical hammer, Mjolnir, his gloves to catch the hammer as it returns, and his belt that doubles his strength is known to all. His chariot is pulled by two black goats who are not friendly; he comes to battle with his wife, Sif, and their two sons, who are also renowned warriors. Then too, comes his servants, one of whom holds Thor's staff Gridarvolar, a powerful talisman. The Spear-Shaker's wife, Frigg, comes to the war in a chariot pulled by two golden boars that are her pets in peaceful times, but now they scowl and snort. Freya, the Goddess of the home, love, and fertility, joins Frigg. She also drives a chariot, hers drawn by two enormous lions.

The Goddess Hel

So comes the war-God Tyr, whose missing hand has been replaced by a metal one made by the dwarfs. He shouts encouragement to the men and Gods as they work to put on their armor and take their places among the gathering horde. Running from out of the halls of Freya and Odin, men in armor come by the thousands.

The Goddess Freya on Her Way to the Final Battle

By now, the host is enormous, yet the All-Father waits for he knows it is still not enough; at length come the forces from Hel; they had the longest journey to make. The daughter of Loki, Hel, is a monster herself; half a living woman but half a corpse blue from death, yet she must come when summoned. She wears no armor nor carries a weapon save the fearsome staff in her hand, which holds an eagle's skull on the tip. A single touch from that rod will make a corpse out of any beast, no matter how fierce.

The captain of her fleet is Baldur, the pure one slain by the one God who would not be there that day for Loki will stay in his prison deep in the earth as he was too unreliable to release, even now. Then too, will come to the fabulous ship named Nagelfar, made entirely out of the trimmed finger and toenails of dead men, some of whom serve as her crew.

When Odin sees that all have come, he will bid the drums sound, and the host will march forth from Asgard. It will take a very long time to march through the gates even though they are as wide as ten ships are long. When they reach the appointed place, the one who is always Glad of War will raise his spear, whereupon his forces will gather on either side of him for many leagues.

When the monsters see the vast army of the All-Father in a deep line stretched leagues across the plain, tens of thousands of warriors, the creatures will grind their teeth and gnash their tusks in anger. The trolls will grunt, rant, and roar, while giant wolves and boars will raise a hideous sound. Hairy brutes will beat their chests as manlike creatures of frost will gibber and slobber adding to the uproar. But the men and Gods will bravely reply with war-like cries and by beating their shields with their weapons. This will overwhelm the noise made by the monster horde. Indeed, they will be alarmed at the vast welling of sound that comes up from the army of Asgard. But only for a short time will they be disconcerted, for soon their anger will return with force enough to make these wild creatures foam at the mouth. And then the battle will begin, but this last contest's victor is not contained in any book or legend as nobody has dared to think of the outcome.

Translated from the original Latin documents containing the <u>Saga of Merila Argisdottar</u> by John Borough of Sandwich, Garter King of Arms, November 1636.

The Goddes Skadi and her pet wolf

Chapter Ten

The Saga of Snorri Skallafreyrsson

The Death of King Ragnar Avenged

[In the 21st year of the reign of King Ragnar of the Danes on the 12th day of Tvirmanodur, I Snorri, son of Freyr, poet to the court of King Ragnar Lothbrok, in the City of Haugen, record for posterity and for my own family the singular portents, signs, and events that I have seen with my own eyes concerning the revenge of the Sons of Ragnar Lothbrok upon the Saxons and other peoples of that island for their execution of their father.]

King Ragnar has been gone for many days now with no news. Queen Aslaug did beg on bended knee for him to stay home and wait another season to raid the Christians on their big island. She told him of her dream of crows circling over his fleet and of fell creatures of the deep feeding on the bones of his men. These words did freeze the souls of all who heard them, including me. It is known that Aslaug has the gift of sight that her father got for killing a dragon and bathing in its blood, and also from her mother, who was a servant of Odin. Yet Ragnar, after giving the Gods his pledge to fight the Saxons that year when he was in Uppsala, could not go back on his oath. Yet he refused his son's permission to accompany him. If it was the will of the Gods that he should die, he was content, yet he would not have his sons share his doom. There was but little cheer in the land when King Ragnar left with his ships. Indeed, his queen was not the only one to fear the result of this raid. Others too had observed the signs, nor was the wife of Ragnar alone in having dreams of circling carrion birds.

The Ghost of Ragnar Lothbrok Sigurdson

One day the morning had not advanced much when a fearsome storm did beat down against the city as Thor repeatedly smashed his hammer against the skulls of the ice giants and other creatures he often battled with. The sky turned black as night; indeed, there was but little light, nor would torches stay lit in the howling wind. For the wind did howl as fell creatures were heard wailing in the distance. Indeed, the whole of the north was dark that evil day. Then came to the throne room Queen Aslaug who this day sat on Ragnar's throne, a thing that she had never done before. Her eyes were red with sorrow and tears as she sat there. She called everyone in the palace to attend her then she announced, with great sobs of grief, that the king was dead; he had been murdered by the Saxons. His ghost had told her this as it made its way to the Hall of Heroes in Asgard.

The Queen then sent for the three Christian priests being held for ransom; two were Saxons, the other a Frank. When they were brought, she had them killed in front of her. Nevermore would priests be ransomed, she declared. If they were captured at sea, as these men were, they would be hung from the mast, for she blamed the priests most of all for the death of Ragnar.

Her son Ivar was the only one of Ragnar's sons at court. He said little but condoled his mother, the Queen. Once I did see a tear fall from his eye, I felt in my heart that a thousand would die for that one tear, for I knew Ivar well. When it was said that Ragnar's other three sons should be told, she said there was but little need to send messengers; they had heard Ragnar's ghost as well, and when the season of raiding drew near, they and their men would be in the city.

Ivar took the building of ships into his own hands. Soon all who could work went to the shipyards to build more longships of war. Dozens of ships were seen rising from the builder's yards, some exceedingly large. They looked like many lean and hungry serpents as they waited, row upon row.

I myself carved many of the dragons that were seen on the prows of these vessels. With the red paint of war mixed in my own blood, I painted the runes of fortune and fame upon every ship. On my own shield I placed powerful signs of protection; revenge was always in my mind at that time for I loved Ragnar, who treated me well. Thrice with his own hands, he gave me my share of the Danegeld.

In the spring of the year, as the raiding time approached, the city was filled with men from all over who hungered to fight the Saxons and their foul dog priests. Men came too because of the famous war captains who would lead the fleet. The most famous was Bjorn Ironsides Ragnarsson, who sailed into port with seven large ships loaded with proven warriors. His brother Vitserk came with fifteen ships from Sweden, and his other brother Sigurd Dragon-Eye brought in many loads of men and supplies from the outer islands. The whole city was one large hive of bees, with the Queen Aslaug handing out pieces of silver to those she saw working the hardest.

Ragnar and Aslaug in Better Times

When the day came to sail, the bay was so filled with ships that one could walk from one side to the other without touching the sea. Other ships were waiting to join on the way. How many ships did we have? Few could guess; indeed, the number was beyond the ability of most warriors to count. I believe it exceeded the great fleet that Bjorn Ironsides had gathered to sail into the sea without tides. Certainly, the ships were much bigger; Vitserk's ship, *The Grim Snake*, carried a hundred men.

The night before we left, Queen Aslaug, along with the sons of King Ragnar, assembled under the open sky in front of the palace. To honor the Gods, they painted their faces and bodies in different colors and wore the skins of wolves and other animals. Drums were beaten, and horns sounded as thousands of people watched. For sacrifice, some ten men, mostly Franks, I think, were taken to a gallows especially constructed for this event. Six were hung on ropes. The others had their heads chopped off, which were used to decorate the entrance to the palace. After the sacrifices were made and the omens were read, which the priests proclaimed to be good, drinking and feasting followed, for everyone knew that for some, this would be their last celebration.

The next morning when the horns sounded, we held our hands over our ears; we were all suffering to some extent from the amount of wine we had drunk the night before. Many stumbled rather than walked as we boarded the ships.

I was with Bjorn Ironsides as he left in his ship *Wolf's Tooth*. As we passed out of the harbor, I could see Queen Aslaug standing on the dock, holding a sword over her head with both hands as she chanted invocations to the Gods. She looked to me to be the very Goddess of War, with her face painted blue, the color of death. She spoke fell words and curses to incite the Gods to assist them against the Saxons, Angles, and others who dwelled in that land. I thought that her petition would be likely granted for one of Odin's names is: *He Who is Glad of War*.

Ten days later, we were at the mouth of the Humber. We saw but little of the Saxons as we sailed up the river, although we could sometimes hear distant horns. The men were so eager for combat that they rowed like demons; indeed, Bjorn had to slow them, or they would lack the energy for hard fighting later. On the afternoon of the third day, we landed our ships on a broad bank with a sandy shore near a grove of trees. This was as far as we could travel by ship, for the Saxons had blocked the river with boats loaded with stones. When we went ashore, the Saxons were waiting with arrows and crossbows, which made things hot for us for a while, but we put them to flight after a sharp fight. They then assaulted us with men on horse with spears; none lived. We swarmed them, pulling them and their horses to the ground.

This was but a pinprick to our host, which now numbered in the thousands. We made camp that night, where we rested from our voyage, eating hotcakes, and drinking mead. The next morning as the drums beat, and the horns sounded, we headed north to the great Saxon city of York, which is a large city; bigger than any in Denmark. We were still some distance from the gates when we saw the high towers of their walls and temples. Christian temples often have towers with bells which they use to summon their God; as we drew nigh, we could hear them clattering. Bjorn and the other captains hoped the Saxons would fight outside their walls. This, of course, they did not do except for the few hundred or so archers and mounted men we saw naught.

When we drew within sight, Bjorn ordered the camp to be made on the top of a nearby hill. Then he summoned a group of captains and jarls and me to ride with him around the city on horses we had captured. We looked hither and thither at the walls and the nature of the ground, with Bjorn noting several points where he thought the defenses to be weak.

The next morning the men were ordered to cut down trees to make ladders and a covered battering ram. I knew Bjorn too well to think he would rely on these means to carry the walls. The Saxons would exact a heavy toll on anyone who tried to take the city by storm. For myself, I had no great desire to climb a ladder only to be greeted at the top by a pot of boiling oil. No, he would think of something else. He was seen deep in conversation with his brothers throughout the day. But whatever he did, it would be done sooner rather than later, for it would be difficult to maintain an army of over three thousand men in the field for any length of time. Supplies would run out and there was always the danger of sickness when so many men are gathered into one place.

On the fifth day after our landing, we were still employed at preparing to storm the main gate to the city. A large ram, which men called *the sow*, was being built just out of bow shot from the walls. When finished, it would consist of a tree trunk hung by chains from a roofed structure on six wooden wheels. There would be when completed, room for about twenty men under the roof; of course, the protective ditch had to be crossed first. Piles of sticks tied together were being assembled for that purpose.

A ditch filled with sticks would be good fuel for fire I thought as I examined it doubtfully, for this was the sort of weapon the Saxons would be looking for. The defenses of the city were designed to resist just such engines of war. As it approached, the defenders would seek to set it on fire and drop heavy stones on it; if it got close to the walls, chains with hooks would attempt to grasp it and pull it over on its side. Or failing that, large metal points on enormous spears dangling from chains would be dropped to make holes in the roof to allow hot oil or flaming pitch to the inside; when it came time to pick men to push this monstrosity, I planned to be far away.

That night the men were told to be ready for anything. I could see small bands of men furtively picking their way around the edge of the camp towards the city. Now I understood part of Bjorn's thinking. Like his father, he was fain to use guile and stealth to accomplish his victories. If he could enter the city in a crafty way, he would save the lives of many.

Some while after the evening meal, large campfires were built in a circle in the middle of the camp. Men were persuaded to beat drums, chant songs, and dance. A part of the story of King Rothgar of the Geats and the monster that terrified his drinking hall was acted out by men wearing horns and other strange garbs to resemble characters from the tale. Of course, this would clearly be seen by the Saxons, who presumably would be mystified by such goings-on. In the night, lit only by fires, it was not easy to see that about half the men were now gone. It took no great thinking on my part to determine where they went. Men would try to scale the walls with hooks and ropes. If only one group was successful, a gate could be opened. Bjorn's men laughed up their sleeves as they watched the dancers and musicians create the distraction. However, as entertained as the Saxons might have been, their sentries were watchful. Nothing was accomplished save the death of a few men. A shipmate of mine, Kettil Stakersson, took an arrow through his neck for his trouble.

Ragnar's Death Avenged

This did not deter Bjorn from trying to find another way to enter the city; often I saw him and his war captains in deep conversation as they walked to and fro before the walls searching for a place that could be pierced; four days later, they made a different sort of attempt. They thought that by attacking the main gate with the sow and ladders, this would divert sufficient strength from the Saxon defenders to allow them to attack the two other gates with smaller battering rams built out of sight and only taken to the gates at the last minute. I was full of doubts about this as the smaller rams were uncovered, making them vulnerable to stones and arrows. When this attack commenced, it was my intention to be far in the rear of my comrades. This was indeed the case, for when the attack was ordered I was onboard one of the ships talking to a friend. When I heard the horns sound, I raised my sword and cheered with the rest, then slowly advanced leaving the more frenzied warriors to run ahead of me.

Of course, the attack failed; the Saxons dropped bundles of burning fagots next to the sow on each side; within a very short time, the sow was being pulled back as the heat began to roast those inside. As for the ladders, the less said, the better. Most were built too short to reach the top of the wall. The ones who did manage to reach the top of the walls were pushed over by long sticks with a fork in the end. All of this was so ridiculous that I couldn't help laughing behind my shield.

The Saxons laughed from their vantage point; Bjorn also laughed heartily as he booted the arses of those responsible for the short ladders. It was then that our men noticed that in an old tower, part of earlier fortifications that were now incorporated into the outer wall, there was a privy that stuck out far enough so that it emptied into the ditch below. Vitserk noticed that there were no bars warding the privy, so if the wooden seat was removed, entry might be gained from below.

A few days later, on a cloudy night, a long ladder was worked into position. It seemed perfect for an agile and thin man to gain entry by this means.

High hopes were entertained for the success of this privy raid; long lines of men waited quietly in the dark for their turn to go up the ladder. A ship captain, Tingol the Lean, was selected for the high honor of quietly removing the wooden seat by stealth, then penetrating the hole. But as it turned out, he got more than he bargained for when Tingol reached the top of the ladder; some ill luck came his way. A guard had just sat to relieve himself, so Tingol got a mighty fart in the face, followed by a large load of excrement. This almost knocked him from the ladder.

As it was, he was forced to descend the ladder as his eyes had been severely fouled. This took place in near-perfect stillness, so there was hope that the guards would not be alarmed. However, this was not the case. The next man who went up the ladder was able to remove the seat and climb up, whereupon a Saxon removed the top portion of his head with an axe. So ended what was later called *The Night of the Big Shit*.

A few days later, Bjorn launched an all-out attack on the city. He held nothing back. First, archers shot flaming arrows over the walls while men with ladders, this time long enough, attempted to scale the walls. The other gates were again assaulted regardless of the losses. But it was the main gate that fell. Bjorn had large iron hooks attached to ship cables made of walrus hide. These he had flung over the gates. When the hooks caught the gate, he had hundreds of men pull on the cables until the gate, with post and hinges included, came crashing down. Even then, the Saxons fought for their lives, for they knew it was useless to ask for quarter. Yet it was for naught; they were attacked at too many places at one time. Our men, maddened by fighting and slaughter, entered the city with swords dripping blood. They killed without mercy all that they found, even those who had value as slaves; even mothers with babes at their breasts had their throats slit. For myself, I went with others to see the big Christian temple where great riches were expected to be found. Others had the same idea as the few priests that were found; most had fled, it seemed, were being made by hot irons to tell where they had hidden the treasures. Their God demands to be served only with silver or gold cups and plates, so there was always plunder to be had among the Christians. Nor were precious metals the only riches to be found; some of these vessels were encrusted with precious stones. Their God also requires that the bones of some of his greatest followers be kept to be used in their magical rites. I found one hidden in a pile of fagots, a toe from a revered follower that was mounted on pure gold set with rubies. Also, a piece of magical wood was kept in a beautiful silver box of the best workmanship.

Later I took two boys I found hiding behind in a merchant's shop and sent them back to be sold as slaves. Such was the personal riches that I had gained thus far. The lack of Christian priests that we found caused great sorrow in our ranks, for they were much blamed for the death of Ragnar. King Aella sent them away as soon as our ships were spotted; their chief priest was supposed to have ridden west seeking assistance.

As for King Aella, I was there when they brought him into the Christian temple along with some of his chief men. He was bloodied and spent from the kicks and blows that he received. He was taken to a peculiar device that the Christians used to make smoke and produce a stench for their God. It was a large wide shallow bucket that burned clumps of a sweet tree resin. I was told that the Christians, who seldom bathed, were a smelly lot. To appease the nose of their God, they would light the resin afire and then swing this stinkpot up and down and around until the smell of the Christian arses was sufficiently disguised to suit their God. I thought a hundredweight of soap could be put to better use. Be that as it may, King Aella was spread and tied to this stinkpot, the stench-producing resin piled on his back, and his clothing set on fire. Then he was pulled up above the heads of our men, who pushed him forward and backward so that he flew above us like a giant eagle of pain crying out in agony. He howled until he could make no more sounds. From that day forward, he was known as *Aella the Eagle*. Then he was taken down, his head cut off, which was put on a spike on the outer wall. His body was thrown into a ditch where men took turns pissing on it. Thus, the first token of revenge for the death of Ragnar was taken.

We decided to hold York as a base from which we would strike out. The men from the western part of Aella's realm made peace with us with rich gifts and much coin. Those to the North of us simply took to their heels, running as fast and as far as their legs would carry them. They thus escaped, but only for a while. The Saxons, indeed, all who dwelled in that land, were in mortal fear of us. They called us *The Great Heathen* Army; to the eyes of the Christians, no doubt we were.

**The Sons of Ragnar Lothbrok
Sigurd Dragon-Eye, Ivar the Boneless,
Vitserk, Bjorn Ironsides, (standing)**

We spent the rest of the summer raiding the areas nearest to York and took all the coin that was to be had in the immediate area. Where coin was lacking, we took provisions and horses. One large village, having but scant provisions and little coin, brought us a number of priests all roped together. They told us that these monks were like leeches feeding upon the sweat of honest farmers; indeed, they were a fat lot. We heartily thanked these people for their gift of monks that we would put to good use and sport. They soon lost their fat as we put them to pulling our wagons like oxen.

Using prisoners, we dug ditches and made our position very strong. We gathered all the horses that we could find so that we could strike out on a quick raid if we needed. We brought in grain and forage to store safely for the winter. This put us in a very good position when the snow began to fall.

As for the Northumbrians, Saxon or not, they fared but ill. One of them, a Jarl named Osbert, sought to seize the crown and hold sway over the rest of the Christians, but he was unpopular, so much so that his own men killed him. Bjorn Ironsides thought it politic that he should name the next king to rule them. The Christians were not pleased with this, but there was little that they could do. Bjorn picked a Saxon thane named Eckbert, who was old and did what he was told. Later he was replaced with Ricksid, a fool, as their king. Then two years later, Ivar the Boneless Ragnarsson took the crown for himself after Bjorn Ironside left to return to Denmark. We spent that winter in York, where we had a very merry time of it and celebrated Yule amid riches, good drink, sport, and much food.

In the spring, we went south to the Kingdom of Mercia, where we defeated their King in several battles. We took the eastern part of the kingdom for ourselves, with Bjorn again using a local thane to rule over their lands for him. We then struck out eastward into the kingdom of the East Angles. In this series of battles, Ivar the Boneless led our forces, and it was he who captured their king after a battle later in the year. Ivar had their King Edmund used for target practice with arrows. I saw this with my own eyes; Ivar handed out silver coins to those who could put an arrow into the King at a far distance.

When Edmund's thanes asked for his body, Ivar played a trick on them. He found a beggar that looked somewhat like Edmund, killed him, marked his body with false wounds, and then put him in the King's clothes. The coffin was then given to his thanes amid great pomp. Later this body was venerated as a saint with miracles being ascribed to the holy relics of Edmund's body. This made Ivar very happy to see the Angles and the Saxons paying homage to the body of a beggar. As for the real body of the king, it was thrown into a river with stones tied to it.

For myself, I was in the entourage of King Ivar, as he was now called, for he took the kingdom of the dead king Edmund as his own. He made our laws their laws; indeed, our system of laws was called the *Dane Law* by the Christians and their payments to us were termed the *Danegeld*. Many battles were to be fought in the future between our people and the Saxons, especially those of Wessex under their King Alfred; rivers of blood were to flow before the death of Ragnar Lothbrok was fully avenged.

Here endeth the tale told by Snorri Skallafreyrsson.

Chapter Eleven

The Source of Magic

By Rollo Weems

Many nineteenth-century esoteric revivalists claimed that the Druids were the authors of ancient magic. They based this on the writings of Julius, called Caesar, of the Julian clan, who wrote about them in his famous *Commentarii de Bello Gallico*. This was later embellished by various romantic writers and pseudo-historians of the Middle Ages and again by various writers and scribblers of our own time. The Druids did, in fact, encompass with their vast learning certain arts and disciplines of magic but they were not themselves the source of magic. No, the magic that flowed from the earth was far older than the Druids.

Others were impressed, and rightly so, by *The Golden Bough* written by the Scottish anthropologist James George Frazer. This massive tome, first published in 1890, chronicled the vast variety of magical use throughout the world, both in ancient and modern times. It was also the biggest blow to organized religion that had ever been struck. According to Frazer all revealed religion was simply updated and recycled versions of much older beliefs. While this new learning didn't make much of a stir at the village kirk it was widely read at Oxford, Yale, and other top universities.

Yet this learned don erred in one respect. While his work showed the universal appeal of magic, he seemed to think that its flowering took place in the warm breezes of the Mediterranean and the Fertile Crescent. Generations of sweating diggers worrying away the dirt that covered the various tells added credence to this view. But those who know the secret of magic understand that it was not born in the lands of those who would later invent spaghetti and pizza any more than being born among the startlingly realistic reflections of Lake Nemi. In fact, magic was already old by the time that the Etruscans (distant ancestors of the mafia) crowned their first king. The earth's power was not a product of the warm breezes in the southern reaches of civilization. No, it was under the sullen skies found much farther North that the magic flowed into the earth mixed with the pure and cold water that bubbled forth from the sacred pool at the foot of the tree of life. In time the bull riders of Crete and the Pharaohs of Egypt would know magic, but it was by other and later means that are not part of this story.

No precise location is known for the origin of this stream although its probable course can be deduced from the effects that it produced. One area of confluence was in the Neander Valley located in what we would now call the Ruhr. Here its influence saved our ancestor's ancestors from extinction during the most recent Ice Age. From thence it found its way a short distance to the Rhine River and from there out into the broad grasslands and forests that would later become the North Sea and the English Channel; for at this time most of the oceans were low; vast amounts of water were still contained in the glaciers. From there it split directions, one arm went north into Scandia, another bearing straight for the isle that was not yet an Isle while yet another angled towards the east. This magic, being magic, did not always follow the course of least resistance; nor did it always flow downhill. Great pools of magic were formed, the first in Less Britain on the coast of Gaul and yet another in Cornwall, and onward until the Isle of Emeralds was engulfed, and then on to Scotia and the islands large and small. During the early Neolithic period, the time reckoned a couple of thousand years before the first pyramids were built, the only people who had gone across the low grass plains were a few intrepid hunters and their families who followed the Rhine as it went northwest. Others came too, outlaws, solitary adventures, and wild men.

This land might have stayed unsettled for another millennium or more if it were not for the magic. Great riches always draw people even if, as in this case, they don't quite understand what sort of riches they were following. They came on instinct; they stayed due to good farmland and an increasingly equitable climate.

The newcomers did find magic. Their methods of obtaining its use were inventive if not well comprehended. Music and poetry could summon it. But so could blood and fire. Early on people learned that magic could be channeled to some extent, or focused, by certain kinds of stone and trees, especially oak, rowan, and yew. It didn't take long before the first circles of stone and wood were built; in time hundreds of them littered the countryside. Others made rude chapels in the dark groves of trees or sacrificed bulls on stone altars hidden in caves.

From early on Gods were named to personify the various aspects that the magic revealed. Did this create Gods? Or would the Gods laugh to hear this question?

The influx of people into England surged and ebbed according to the climate and politics of the times. But safe to say that by the second millennium before the start of the Common Era there was a thriving population that may well have exceeded a hundred thousand people. Many settled on the east coast in what would be later called Anglia after the German tribe that settled thereabouts. This term was later corrupted to become England. This was fortunate because the next wave of immigrants was the tribe of the Geruchenne; roughly meaning stinking people without soap.

Here these Neolithic valley dwellers settled the banks of the tidal estuaries following the river courses ever inland. By this time, they practiced a rather sophisticated type of agriculture which they developed about as far as they could without metal to make plows with. This was supplemented of course by the age-old practices of hunting and fishing. The rivers were vital to their lives and soon became busy trade routes; they were also rich in magic.

Post-Roman Scandinavia

Among those who sought to harness magic for good were others of much less lofty ambition. Nowhere were dishonest people more concentrated among the errant children of the land than those who claimed to be able to foretell the future. With the possible exception, of course, of those who steal chickens. Worse, some of these crooked visionaries were lunatics who decorated their long locks with animal bones and smeared their noses with ashes or owl dung. Curiously the grotesque appearance of these imposters, coupled with their rank smell, only served to make their raving more believable to the credulous.

The land was full of those who read omens in animal livers or by signs in the sky. Others looked at palms or threw bones made out of fox knuckles, while yet other seers consulted the flames of cook fires or the hides of skunks. Of the future, they knew naught. Yet they tended to be shrewd in gauging the credulity of their customers and expert in telling people what they wanted to hear. Like every charlatan that has come before or since they were experts in the use of weasel words that hedged prophecies in vague terms that could mean just about anything. Like the fake prophets that operate today, they claimed hindsight as foresight and would tell all who would listen of their supposed advanced knowledge of important events. Failures were ascribed to the inability of the hearer to comprehend the true meaning of the prophecy. Or a seer would claim that those who carped about the accuracy of the prophecy were in the employ of a rival who sought to discredit him.

The honest in this curious profession were few, a very few. These relied on an intuition fed by a genuine inner flame of magic. The very best of these had an uncommon intelligence that could discern within the *Sight* a true knowledge of what will be or could be. Even fewer in number than genuine seers were those who had the ability to use magic as a tool or a weapon. For this took an inherent ability to summon magic at will and the mental capacity and the discipline to focus it. How it was then used depended on the ability and the experience of the user. Most who had learned the discipline of magic had also learned something about themselves and the world that they lived in. They had no interest in gathering up large sums of gold nor did they wish to wear a crown. But always there are a few who have a great hunger to dominate others. Bending others to their will is seen by them as the natural order and, full of self-justification, they will stop at nothing to get their way. Magic by itself knows neither good nor evil. Like rain, it falls on the just and unjust alike.

It takes a lot to disturb the flow of magic but with enough human activity, it could be done. And was in fact done in what we now call the Age of Migrations. Between the years 375 C.E. and 700 C.E. whole populations picked up and left for other locations both near and far. The Lombards for instance, traveled all the way from northwest Germany to Italy which at that time was seriously depopulated following the fall of Rome and depredations of tribes like the Goths. All of this was a great boon to later historians as it gave them plenty to write about. But those living in those turbulent times would have been unlikely to join in the enthusiasm of later academics.

All of this movement had the effect of stirring the powers that flowed unseen in the earth. Magic, whose use was always very unpredictable became more so. Only those who possessed a rare and penetrating insight, as well as a strong sense of inner discipline, could use it safely.

Used by such people magic could bring strength and harmony to a culture. Used by evil, wild, or insane men or women it could bring about an apocalypse of evil and unquiet graves, always the harbingers of pestilence, despair, and black summers. While the many stone circles and later literature enshrined the British Islands as a preeminent source of magic it did not in truth, surpass the portion given to those lands that border what we now call the Baltic Sea. Unfortunately for later historians, practitioners of magic in those parts left few things to remember them by. Those savants cared little for memorializing their existence with carvings or slabs of stone. No, their rites were practiced in the dark, often in secret and sacred groves of the forest or in hidden hollows. It was the beating hearts of living creatures that excited their interest. We know very little of these people save that their practices and revels were shielded by the dark of night. It must be admitted that word has come down from the ages that some of the Gods worshiped in the far eastern states of the Baltic were of an exceptionally cruel nature. It is said that they required excessive payment for their favor and gifts. Yet it cannot be denied that as dubious as their methods were reputed to have been, the results were sometimes impressive. It was among these nameless people that the fell curses of the shade life were first used. A way was found to ensnare the body and soul of a person in a state in which the person was both dead and alive at the same time. This paradox is impossible in the natural world of course. Nor should something so abominable have been invented using magic. Yet it happened; later a way was found, fortunately, to defeat these terrible curses.

As for the Danes, the Swedes, Geats, and petty kingdoms of Norway that existed in this period, magic was known, respected, even treasured as a precious commodity like gold or silver. Yet the best magic never seemed to come from home. The wealthy vied with each other to enlist the services of magical savants. Often, they came from the Rus or outlandish regions whose names were otherwise unknown in the north. Of this, no group was more powerful, or respected, than the rune cutters.

For some reason never understood, the alphabet of the north known as runes proved to be a very effective way to carry magic. This didn't mean that every man who set up shop to carve runes had magic. Most had no magical ability whatsoever. The majority of the roadside memorials to departed friends or family were made by artisans of this class. While men of rune magic could, and sometimes did, make such ordinary stones a good part of their more advanced work resides underground and therefore unable to be appreciated by the living.

The vile sorcerers who had the ability to use curses to make the dead their servants were never many. Thankfully no more than a handful had ever mastered the complex nature of the curses, whose exact wording was deeply hidden so that for most times this was never an issue. The ones who did manage to control the dead, who were called necromancers, were of course completely insane. Only a deeply flawed mind would want to engage in something as repellent as creating shade creatures. And if their mind was not unhinged when they started out it would soon be warped by the very magic that is summoned. Indeed, tales were told about one necromancer who made a terrible mistake in casting a spell. Instead of forcing the spirit of a departed soul into perpetual slavery, he made himself into a shade. Yet cautionary stories of this sort didn't completely keep people from trying. The lure of power has always been too attractive for everyone to resist.

But the runes of power cut into the stone at night, without the use of metal, mixed with the blood of one who carries magic, can defeat a necromancer. The skill of the rune cutter, a true master of the magical craft, can do many other things as well depending on his inner strength and intelligence. A special lineage can make a difference too, sometimes a great difference.

Yet questions will always remain. For what purpose is this power to be used? Temptations will present themselves as often as the moon rises. Will the carrier of magic by the strength of character resist temptation? None can say until they themselves are put to the test.

Chapter Twelve

A Tale of Slack the Hardheaded

Fate Will Always Win Out

In the old country of the Vandals there lived a farmer by the name of Stump who was unknown except among his nearest neighbors for he was a very modest and quiet man who never did anything of interest. He lived on his nondescript farm with a wife who was as silent and uninteresting as he was. It was said that the raven Muginn once stopped here to collect news but found so little that he fell asleep on a branch; a fact he related to the All-Father that night.

As it was Odin had an errand to run in that vicinity a few weeks later so he paid a visit to that farm. The man Stump was dull and quiet 'twas true but he obeyed the law of hospitality and served food and drink to the All-Father, who came in the guise of an old man who was, as usual, dressed meanly in a worn grey robe belted with a rope and a wide-brimmed hat of the same color. The woman was as quiet as her man, yet her face was kind enough; the All-Father sensed that she was lonely, very likely the result of being childless. So, when the man turned his head away the old man spit in his beer.

That night the woman was shocked to see that her man came to her in his most ardent manly state; it had been some time since he had shown any lust at all towards her. She didn't know why but she suspected that his frenzied embraces would result in a baby, which nine months later was the case. So it was that the boy named Slack Stumpson came into history. Young Slack was the pride of his parents although he failed to distinguish himself in any way. He was of average height, neither fast nor slow in games, and did his chores with the same lack of enthusiasm that most boys show. Just as he was coming into manhood his father took him to the priest, as was the custom, to have his future forecast.

Slack Stumpson

The priest cut the boy's finger enough to get out a couple of drops of blood that he dribbled onto a cup of cooking oil. Then, after a deep breath and an even deeper frown he reached into his bag of divining bones and cast them a number of times in growing astonishment. He then gave the father his coin back and told him to depart and not come back.

"This is the work of Loki, the trickster, and I'll not be part of it!" he said in disgust. But after seeing the look on the father's face and his clear astonishment he said, "the portents show that this lad will live long and die wealthy, yet he will make the Gods roar with laughter! But it simply cannot be that any boy born in this deepest arse hole of the world could amuse anyone, much less the Gods. The demons take me but there is very little to smile about in these parts."

A couple of years later the people in the area, who were unlucky enough to live within a few miles from the sea, were attacked by a neighboring king who sought to augment his supply of food by stealing from his neighbors. Slack, who had been taking a nap behind the barn (when he was supposed to have been in the fields working) woke to find a man busy stealing their best nanny goat which infuriated him to the extent that he grabbed a nearby flail and beat the man's brains out with it. He then cautiously peeked around the corner of the barn where he saw, to his horror, a group of enemy warriors sitting in front of this house eating their sausages and bread while drinking their beer. He could see other men in the distance, so he knew that this was a large raid. As for his parents, they apparently fled in the farm wagon which was still loaded with ground flour from the miller. His natural path of escape blocked he had no option but to go towards the sea where he looked for a place to hide. But he was frustrated in this for the looters were now returning to their ships with such booty as they were able to collect. As it turned out the people were able to save enough food to avoid starvation that winter, but nobody could tell, at least for the moment, what had become of Slack Stumpson. As it was the lad was able to sneak aboard a large vessel where he crawled below deck to hide among the bales, boxes, and barrels of looted provisions. It was his intention to sneak back on shore that night but by then the ship was far out of sight of land.

Feeling ill from the motion of the ship which was really rather mild he went up on deck by crawling out of a hatch covered only with an old tarp. Before he could reach the rail though he vomited a number of times, as it turned out he did so onto the sandals of a sleeping sailor. This gave him an idea for his mind was now filled with hatred for these brutal killers and thieves who now slept on the deck. Lowering his rump over a cap of another sleeping sailor he filled it to the brim with half-liquid stools so smelly that a walrus would turn aside from the stench; after which he wiped his badly soiled ass off with the cloak of yet another man leaving several long stains in the process. Then, casting his eyes about by the light of the moon that shone down on the exhausted sailors and sleeping warriors he spied a covered bucket with a ladle next to it; no doubt this was water for the thirsty crew. After drinking his fill, he added a liquid of his own which caused him to smile as he merrily peed away a very full bladder. Then he returned the way that he came by the hatch.

He slept as soundly as he could until the morning light awoke the crew. The cursing was in his own language, so he didn't need an interpreter to tell him of the varied and terrible oaths that were being exchanged above his head. No doubt accusations were made and answered as the crew dealt with the results of his mischief. Of course, he was beginning to suffer from the lack of food and drink but not for long since they made port that same afternoon. As soon as he was able to sneak a look from out of the hatch, he knew that he was in a neighboring land ruled by King Mope whom they had often fought with.

The docks were filled with guards who watched the workers who were unloading ships, so our hero just grabbed a small barrel, of beer it turned out, and when nobody was looking, he carried it onto the pier like the others were doing. This bravado was entirely successful; just when he was looking for a way to escape, he recognized a boy from his village who had been captured and put to work. He joined the other boy in carrying loot from the ships and, when nobody was looking, they talked and made their plans.

The other boy who was only a year older than Slack said that he had overheard the men talking to each other on the voyage. One reason for the raid they said was to gather supplies and animals for a big celebration that their king was having to mark his tenth year of rule; before he was king it was his uncle who sat on the throne, but he was treacherously killed on a hunt by his nephew who shot him in the back with an arrow. Today they would start with bearbaiting; they had four large bears from the far north in cages, famished of course, after the bears had been sufficiently angered by dogs, they would be fed several people whose lands the King wanted for his own. The citizens would be edified by watching these unfortunate people being chased around a stockade by these beasts before being eaten alive. Following that the principal men and women of the region would have to wear wooden masks carved to represent the ancestors of the King as they sacrificed animals. It was said that if the King was feeling generous, which was seldom, he would allow these nobles to join him in a grand feast, presumably without the masks on.

Unknown to the King his festivities were being watched by some very special visitors; the ruler of Asgard sat in a tree in the guise of an owl while others of the Gods readied themselves for the spectacle in similar disguises; Freya for instance, took the form of a woodchuck while Frigg made herself into a hare. The Gods were aware of the special fate of young Slack but not the particular manner that it would be expressed. And if the King's reputation suffered that was fine with them, for he had no friends among the Gods.

Perhaps the mere presence of the Gods inspired Slack to superior methods of sowing discord for his mind that day proved extremely agile. In later life, he was able to point to this day with great pride as it showed to all that he was much more than the offspring of dull people in a boring land.

It was the plan of Slack and his countryman Dikit, to cause enough disturbances to lure the guards away from the ships so that they could steal a small craft and escape. After much discussion, they made a plan, the first part of which was to locate the carved wooded masks that represented the sacred ancestors of the king. These were made with great care and precision with eyeholes to see through and ribbons that stretched behind the head to tie it on with. After some searching, they found them in an unguarded wagon parked outside the amphitheater. Acting like they were merely doing their jobs the boys jumped into the wagon, clucked to the horses, and drove off. They didn't go far though, just to the stockade where the animals awaiting sacrifice were being kept. There was only one lone guard here who walked over to the wagon to see what was going on, as Slack engaged him in conversation Dikit beat him over the head with a club of wood. They hid the body as well as they could before turning their attention to the animals.

They took the ancestral masks and tied them onto the heads of the goats and sheep except for the two that they tied to the tails of the white oxen. They made sure that the masks were tied on tightly; Slack couldn't help laughing when he saw the animal eyes peering back at him out of the family mask icons. Then they opened the gate and shooed the animals towards the center of the town where King Mope awaited this solemn procession. It should be noted that several subjects of his who came across these beasts suffered in various degrees to the exhaustion caused by excessive laughter. When a while later it was reported to the king what had happened, he almost foamed from his mouth in anger. His men were not nearly as angry as he was; in fact, many were forced to carefully place their hands over their mouths to cover their feelings. While the King sped off to investigate this outrage Slack and Dikit made their way to the caged bears that were on wagons outside the house where their keepers lived. The men were inside eating as the starving animals outside were nearly mad with hunger. It drove the poor beasts to distraction to smell the food that their hated keepers were stuffing themselves with.

More quickly than it takes to tell about it the lads opened the cages and left on horseback as the big animals made straight for the house; they were hungry and had scores to settle so they never gave Slack and Dikit a single glance. Soon loud screams were heard coming from the house. A couple of the King's men, hearing the commotion, ran into the house to see what was going on; moments later they were to be seen running out at full tilt as a bear chased them. Since bears can move very fast for short distances their fate was not a pleasant one. Word of the escaped bears began to be heard in the town making the people run to and fro in a panic. The boys left their horses and joined the bleating throng who ran in every direction as they heard distant screams coming from those who had been caught by the snarling animals. They ran to the edge of the harbor where they found the building where the stolen loot had been stored. The guards heard the tumult going on nearby when a goat wearing one of the King's ancestral masks over its face ran by. The men looked at each other in amazement, grabbed their spears, and made their way to find the source of the disorder.

The boys found the shack that the guards lived in, so they were able to get flint and iron to make a fire then they went into the storehouse of King Mope and set it ablaze in several places. Then they hid behind a pile of old barrels and waited for the fire alarm to be raised. A few minutes after smoke began to drift skyward a horn was heard followed a short time later by a loud bell. The guards, with the exception of those who had bears to deal with, came running; this left the docks deserted. The boys then stole a small sailboat to make good their escape with. As it turned out the lads made it home where their story made them into local heroes.

As for King Mope, things went badly, for when he saw the body parts strewn about by the bears and oxen with his ancestral icons tied to their tails he went wild with anger; when he saw his storage building go up in flames, he literally tore handfuls of hair from out of his head. He ran into the building to rescue a bag of gold that he had hidden but at that moment the roof fell in putting an end to his rule. When the people found his bones in the rubble, they threw them into the harbor for they were glad to be rid of him.

As for the Gods, nothing is known but it is suspected that they all had a good number of laughs as they witnessed the demise of King Mope.

When the King of the Vandals heard of how Slack had managed to kill off a dangerous and hated enemy, he named him jarl of the district and gave him both land and gold. He married a rich woman of that region who brought much wealth into the family and bore him many fine children. Thus, the words of the seer who saw him in his youth were proved to be true.

Chapter Thirteen

The Resurrection of Bjorn Ironsides

Bjorn Wishes for a Christian Burial

All the sons of King Ragnar of the Danes achieved fame as great warriors. Vitserk, for instance, as a youth surpassed even his father in his ability to throw the spear and axe with accuracy and distance. Later when he led his people against the Saxons of England he showed not only bravery, which was common enough among the Danes but intelligence which was much less common.

His brother Ivar, called *Ivar-the-Boneless* because the bones in his legs were merely gristle, also became a great leader of the warrior host. Due to his infirmity, he could not stand in the shield wall but instead gave orders from his litter of spears. Ivar was very intelligent and a competent leader who became monstrously rich, but he had a cruel streak in his nature which caused prudent men to be wary in their dealings with him.

Sigurd, called *Sigurd Dragon-Eye* because of a small defect in his right eye that looked like a dragon, was the closest to his mother Queen Aslaug who as a maid was styled *Princess Aslaug of the Swedes*. Indeed, the golden dragon-shaped fleck in his eye was a reminder that her father, King Sigurd, had killed the dragon Fafnir which made him a hero in the sagas. Yet of equal fame was her mother, Brunhildi, who was a servant of the All-Father in her own saga. After reaching manhood he became a Jarl in Sweden who looked after his mother's lands in the country. Yet he joined his father when Ragnar went raiding.

But the most famous of King Ragnar Lothbrok's sons was Bjorn, whom his father named *Ironside*s because in his first battle although surrounded by many foes not a single blade could reach him. He was a large man, bigger in fact than King Ragnar who was a man of considerable size; he was also the only man in the Kingdom that was equal to his father in combat. But he was not only his father's equal in size and physical ability he was also like him in his ability to lead and draw other men to his side for he was known to be honest, forthright, generous, and a deep thinker. Also, much like his brother Ivar, he was crafty which the Northmen always valued as a leader. Indeed, if a leader could get what he wanted by guile it was considered even better than winning it in battle since men's lives were not spent. Another trait that he shared with his father was his love of adventure and the exploration of new territories and peoples.

After raiding the Saxons on their big island to the west several times and capturing large amounts of gold and silver besides the usual slaves, supplies, and other goods a traveler sold Bjorn a bit of painted cloth that he had taken from the villa of a rich Frankish merchant that he and his men had looted. He wasn't sure what it was, for none of them had ever seen a map in their lives, but he eventually determined that it was a depiction of what would be later known as the Mediterranean Sea. This was later confirmed to be the case when it was shown to captured Christian priests who had much to tell him as their backsides were prodded with hot irons. One of the priests who was fully motivated by Bjorn's men offered to give up Christianity and guide him to the lands shown on the map. He claimed that he was taken to a monastery as a boy because his parents had too many mouths to feed, and he hated it yet there was no alternative.

Bjorn spent the winter planning his expedition into what was called *the sea with no tides.* He had word sent word out to his estates and all of Daneguard and also to his mother's many family members among the Swedes. Nor did he neglect to inform the rulers in Hordaland, Agder, and Rogaland who were all related to his wife Gunhildi.

By the time the ice cleared from Kattegat, the sea was full of ships heading to join Bjorn Ironside's quest. Absent was his father and brother

Ivar who were busy harrying the Franks and Frisians; however, Vitserk and Sigurd hastened to stand beneath his banner.

The ships were too many to count yet it is not an empty boast to say that there were almost two hundred of them; all of them containing the best manhood that the north can gather. The night before they sailed was talked about for generations afterward as being a great spectacle of both noise, fun, and drunkenness.

Bjorn's mother, Queen Aslaug who was always careful to give the Gods their due planned to give sacrifices unto the Gods; she called for volunteers for this honor but to her surprise, none came forward. She had to make to with several men who were found guilty of cheating on their taxes and while this was not the best material for such an occasion it was the best that could be done. One of them was hung, another decapitated and the third stabbed through his liver; all to the appreciative cheers of the crowd. With the religious ceremony complete the warriors and townspeople of Haugen spent the rest of the night in song and drinking. Very few fights were reported since the men knew that in the near future, they would have all of the fighting that they could stomach.

The first part of the voyage went well enough; they paused to extort money and provisions on the coast of Frankia; the poor citizens of what later would become France took one look at the fleet of Bjorn and gave them everything that they had. But the further down the west coast of Frankia they went on their way to what would later be called Gibraltar the more apprehensive the men became. And when Ironside was told by his captive former priest that upon entering this strange sea they would encounter men with black skin, whom he called *Moors* he thought that the former Christian had lost his mind. But when they put ashore on what is now the southern coast of Spain, they found out that he was right.

There was no opposition to their landing, so the raiders took their time when it came to gathering supplies and plundering the local cities. Indeed, the riches found were so great that the Norse went deeper into this strange land than would be prudent. For their troubles they got a good punch in the snoot when the Emir of the province returned from the north where they had been fighting the Christians; he gave the Norse a good hiding. Ironside's forces had never been up against fully trained soldiers before–they took to their heels back to their ships as fast as their legs would carry them. Those who didn't run fast enough ended up as decorations as they hung from local trees.

Of course, the Viking leaders got much loot and wealth, and slaves. As a side note, it should be related that Moorish captives ended up back in Norway where they were such a wonder that people walked miles to see them. Ironsides was offered large amounts of money for them, but he refused to sell his valuable trophies.

Then they sailed to Italy in order to attack the Pope for they wanted to kill the head of the Christians almost as much as they wanted to gain treasure. On the way they paused at various islands including Malta for supplies and tribute.

When Bjorn Ironsides, Vitserk, and Sigurd Dragon-Eye got to the coast of the Italians they sailed down the coast until they came to a city that they thought could only be Rome. It had buildings made of exquisitely polished stone that stood high enough to rival anything found in Asgard. When the brothers stood high in the prow of their boat and looked at the palaces and wide public ways it took their breath away. Never had they seen, or even imagined, such splendor. There was a problem though: the city was surrounded by a wall thick and high. Such a wall could be easily defended by only a few men.

They drooled over this like wolves would if they saw a flock of sheep. Sigurd spent much time in thought and in close conversation with his brother. According to Bjorn, they schemed for an entire night, nor could a single jug of wine satisfy their thirst.

The following day they sent a messenger to the wall of the city. He wore around his neck a large Christian cross that they had stolen earlier in their voyage. The messenger kept talking in the language of the Franks until a priest appeared on top of the wall and spoke to him in the same language. Soon the priest was following the envoy of the brother back to the ship. For he had been told that his chieftain wanted instruction in the

Christian religion! When the priest arrived on board the vessel, he found Bjorn on a sickbed. The priest spoke to him for a long time, and I should say also that his crew was very receptive to the priest, some even making the Christian sign as he walked by them. At length, Bjorn was baptized. He told the priest that as sick as he was, he would now return to his home to spread the good news of the Christians. The priest was satisfied with that and was allowed to return to his city. A few hours later the fleet sailed out of the harbor, presumably on their way home.

But the ships returned two days later with the sad news that Bjorn Ironside had died but before doing so he had requested that he received a Christian mass and burial among the faithful of the city that had baptized him. His body, wrapped in blankets on a litter carried by four stout men, was brought forward into the city with a couple of dozen of his most devoted friends and brothers, all virtual giants compared to the rather short Italians; this amazed the people but as none of them were armed they were allowed inside the gates. The rest of the men, which were many, stayed outside the walls weeping and lamenting for their fallen captain. Slowly the body of Bjorn was brought inside the church. Many priests were there chanting incantations while the bishop, who the brothers thought was head of the Christian priests called a *Pope* stood at the altar to receive this departed Christian. All went well as songs were sung and smelly things were burned to provide smoke and stench which for some reason their God must have on these occasions.

However, when the body reached the foot of the altar something very unfortunate happened. As the Bishop walked down the steps to sprinkle some holy piss on the body when Sigurd, who was standing on the bottom of the steps, took a hidden dagger from under his cloak and plunged it into the belly of the bishop causing him to howl like a braying ass. At the same time as that Bjorn, not nearly as dead as was thought, leaped from the litter, and taking a sword from the pile that he had lain on, began to lay about in all directions killing a priest at every thrust. Soon all was confusion as the people ran bleating and yammering like frightened sheep. The other crewmen took swords and ran to the city gates. The people scattered in front of them as panic took hold. Once the gates were opened the city was plundered.

The priests did not fare well; some were tied to the inside of the large bells that were hung in the tower, when the bell ropes were pulled, they made a sound that delighted the men of the ships. It took several days to collect all of the slaves that would be taken to be sold and also to carry all the gold back to the ship. When they left the ships were very low in the water. Not all made it back for Bjorn and his brothers had to fight a hard battle with the Moors but those who did return were rich beyond reckoning. All the time they thought they had plundered Rome itself.

It was not until they returned home that they found themselves befooled for the city they had sacked was nowhere near Rome.

Chapter Fourteen

Ragnar Gets a Bride

Guile Can Win a Battle and Sometimes a Bride

By the time Ragnar, son of King Sigurd Ringson of the Danes, reached the age of sixteen he towered over other boys his age nor was he in any way deficient in dexterity or nimbleness for there were none in Zealand who could beat him in wrestling. Indeed, such was his prowess in athletic competition that at the annual All-Thing, the yearly folkmoot, he defeated all competitors of any age in throwing the spear.

To his father the King, he was a source of great pride for not only was he showing the signs of becoming a great warrior but displayed the mental abilities to become a great king.

He was also considered by the maids of the island and all others who came into contact with him to be the most handsome boy in the kingdom. It's said that young women became so weak in the knees when they saw him passing by that they could scarcely remain on their feet. But Ragnar took but little heed of the island's pulchritude as he was already pledged to be married to the beautiful and virtuous Thora, daughter of King Hopp Thorson, the king of Agder, a large and rich province on the southern coast of Norway. But nobody called this haughty king anything other than King Shortlegs because of his diminutive stature. Also, nobody ever called him that to his face for fear of his anger which was known to be explosive.

Ragnar had met Thora on a previous visit when her family came to the Dane capital at Haugen. She was a great beauty to be sure but quite a contrast to Ragnar. Where he was tall and fair, she was of a middling height with dark raven hair. King Sigurd and his wife Queen Helga often on what sort of grandchildren this couple would produce. When the wedding arrangements were being made King Sigurd couldn't help but notice the lack of enthusiasm shown by his colleague King Shortlegs. It seemed that since his wife's death he had become more and more dependent on his daughter to manage the household duties for him as well as becoming his chief advisor. He loved her dearly; in fact, he seemed to dote on her. This of course seemed understandable of course as it was said he missed his departed wife deeply.

But then rumors began to be heard from merchants and rovers that King Shortlegs might renege on the marriage agreement that he had made with King Sigurd. It was said that the King of Rogaland, Ingjald Ogvaldsson, who bordered the lands of King Shortlegs on the west, had made an offer of marriage to his son; an offer said to be more lucrative. However, some considered this to be a ruse on the part of King Shortlegs to keep his daughter at his side for a few more years as she had become invaluable to him in running his kingdom.

When such rumors reached the ears of King Sigurd, he didn't know what to think but nonetheless he decided to find out. He had ways of getting information in every land that could possibly cause him trouble; even among the Franks and Saxons, there were men, and women too, in his pay. He sent out word to his sources in both Agder and Rogaland to see what could be learned on this matter. A few months later a sea captain who worked as a mercenary to guard merchants came to him with information of the most distressing sort.

The ship captain, Thor Thorson, has in his employ a woman, a very intelligent young woman in fact, who worked in a brothel in Jondal who opened her ears besides other parts of her anatomy and by chance was told that King Shortlegs had decided to marry his daughter to the Prince of Rogaland, who was according to rumor every bit as unimpressive as his father. This callow and reportedly indolent youth was a far cry from the handsome and manly Ragnar Sigurdson. According to this same rumor, Thora took this decision with an ill-grace causing her father to keep her behind locked doors lest she should flee.

King Sigurd was flummoxed by this news and knew not what to do. He itched to call for his jarls and warriors and sail to Agder and put this petty king under the sod for this insult. But the season for raiding was almost over and by the time he could summon his forces there would be ice in the fjords. And then too there was the question of spilling so much blood over a question of honor. Yet the King scowled when he told his son the bad news which he was pretty certain was true although so far, he had heard nothing from King Shortlegs himself.

Ragnar was in a rage at the ill news as he barged and pounded his fists on a table in the great hall. He said nothing but those who knew him, which were quite a few as even at a young age he had the ability to attract the best and brightest men to his side, didn't think he would let this pass without action; most of them began to pack for a sea voyage. In this Ragnar didn't disappoint them for early the second day after he heard the news from his father, he slipped out of Haugen early in the morning with a picked crew of supporters bound for the sea lane of Kattegat and then continue west to Agder. Of course, he said nothing to his father before taking the fastest and newest ship in the fleet, *Shield-Breaker*, which had room for all of the eighty men that Ragnar took with him.

In public, King Sigurd condemned this action albeit feebly for in his heart he knew that if he were Ragnar, he would have done the same thing. In fact, he was filled with pride that his son had left and taken with him many of the foremost men on the island. He could not imagine what the outcome would be, yet he understood that the Gods always favored the brave and the bold.

As for his son he'd been busy since he spoke with his father in attempting to learn what he could about the capital of King Shortlegs and where he would most likely find the maid Thora. As he questioned those who had been there, especially recently, much was heard but little was decided. Ragnar declared that they would move in stealthily to spy out the land and fortifications before deciding what to do.

The weather was unfavorable which was not unusual at that time of the year when temperatures began to fall dramatically at night. The ship's crew were all used to such nasty tricks that the weather could heap upon them and came with sealskin coats and caps with boots waterproofed with the oil of minks and otters. Fur-lined mittens were worn by the men at the oars but even so, many of them yearned to be sitting in front of a fire with a cup of warm mead in their hand. But as much as they hankered for the warmth of home every man here was ready to do his duty; many said that as this was likely to be Ragnar's first battle, they yearned to be a part of it so as to have a story to tell their children someday.

Their ship went up a narrow river on a small and uninhabited island within easy sight of Askoy the main island where King Shortlegs had built his stronghold. This fortress was located atop a rise of land overlooking several villages and the port. Ragnar wanted to spy out the land before deciding what to do but his size prevented him from mingling with inhabitants pretending to be just another farmer. Fortunately, the fertile minds of his followers were equal to the occasion. One of his men, of short stature, shaved his beard off and dressed as an old woman, an ugly old woman of course, whilst another man who was a bit taller would pretend to be her husband. Ragnar was doubtful when he heard of this plan yet when he was shown the false couple, he found them to be very convincing. That night they took the ship's skiff across to the main island to reconnoiter the lair of King Shortlegs. While they were gone the crew replenished their casts of water, ate the last of the fresh bread from home, and drank heated wine to drive away from the cold. The following evening the false couple returned with some interesting stories to tell.

Because their accent was different, they pretended to be from Finnstadt which was a good decision since few people have ever been able to discern exactly how Finns are supposed to sound. They said they were intending to look for work on a farm, but they had been put off by rumors of war and wondered aloud if there was any truth to those rumors.

When the spies returned the following evening, they had much to say. Their main line of questioning proved only one thing: that if you ask ten residents of the Norse any question you are liable to get ten different opinions in reply. The question was still useful for it opened the way for other things to be heard, and indeed much was said as the people of the village closest to where King Shortlegs proved garrulous.

As Ragnar heard the many things that his spies had told him he was aware that while the people generally liked King Shortlegs they were mystified by his behavior. In the last six months, he'd become reclusive and wary. He had hired more guards for his estate which was by now a fortress that was solid and stout enough to give pause to even a commander of a great host. It was ideally located on the top of a hill that had three sides warded by wooden walls made out of tree trunks and topped by guard towers. The fourth side had a thick stone wall with a gate made of oak held in place with a crossbeam so heavy it took two men to put it in place. Flanking the gate were two small stone towers with arrow slits that promised a hot time for any attacker. The conundrum of how to get in, and then escape with young Thora in tow, caused the crew to pull their beards in a collective effort to come up with a plan. As difficult as this problem was Bjorn knew that his people had always, given enough time, found solutions to vexing problems. His faith in his people seemed to be rewarded after Stein Nilsson, a member of the crew and the most notorious prankster and liar in the entire north, talked with Bjorn and other leaders over a butt of good wine.

Two days later the ship sailed to the closest large town which was Grimstad, a day's sail up the coast, where they bought many curious items that included cloth, various dyes, and paint.

A few days later . . . King Shortlegs was sitting in his great hall with his retainers talking to a visiting Jarl from upcountry when a breathless servant burst in telling him that a very unusual ship, with a hull painted red and sail of the same color, had just docked in the harbor. In a short time, the King with the short legs (and at the moment wide eyes) was standing on top of his wall with his friends looking toward the harbor watching as the passengers from this strange vessel disembarked.

The King recognized priests when he saw them (which was seldom since he was overdue for his once-every-nine-years visit to Uppsala) for there was no mistaking them. All of them were distinguished looking with their flowing beards, shaved heads inked with runes, and of course the grey tunics that they wore; they also darkened the sockets of their eyes with soot. The crew with them were not priests yet they honored the Gods by painting their faces in various colors. To see a spectacle like this outside of the Temple of the Gods in the north of Swedeland was unheard of and King Shortlegs was at a loss for words which was out of character for him to say the least. The procession of these professional worshipers of the Gods and the ship's company lost no time in walking up the path to the King's residence where they were met at the gate by the King himself.

"Hail King Hopp favored son of the Almighty and Infernal Gods! Odin himself instructed us to come here from Uppsala to take counsel with you. And to drink your fine beer and eat your pork which is said to be second to none! All Hail King Hopp Thorson of Agder, a true man of the Gods!" Thus, spake Stein Nilsson, the false head priest, who was so convincing that Ragnar found himself wanting to believe it. The King ordered quarters found for the priests and their men and that evening a feast would be held in their honor. He was of course bursting with curiosity to find out why these men had come here but he was forced to act according to etiquette that compelled him to wait.

One person who was not totally deceived by all of this blather was his daughter who looked down skeptically from where she stood on the wall above the gate. She'd been around warriors all of her life and could tell by their bearing and gait that there were no priests to be found in the throng that passed beneath her. Her first inclination was to warn her father lest they should all be murdered in their sleep. But she hung back thinking that perhaps there was more to this than she thought. Her thinking was proven right for just then a youth walked below her she could see that he had neglected to dye a patch of hair on the center of his head; this could only be seen from above because he was tall. And despite the blue and red paint on his face, she had a very good idea of who he might be. She had never forgotten the handsome looks of her fiancé, in fact, she had thought of little else since she arrived back in Askoy the previous year.

The feast that night was the best that the sweating cooks were able to arrange on short notice, yet it was not lacking in variety for there were beefsteaks, duck, chicken, lamb, and trout with mounds of fresh bread and potage. And of course, barrels of beer and some very strong spiced wine. The guests as well as King Shortlegs and his retinue made a fierce attack upon the viands to the extent that a person outside the great hall might think, from the sounds of the knives, that some rare evening instruction in swordplay was going on inside. As soon as the sharp edge of their appetites were satisfied somewhat King Shortlegs called for quiet.

"It is years without reckoning since we've had visitors from the Temple at Uppsala. I feel I must inquire if all goes well with the Gods and those in his service?"

"Things go apace as they can," replied Stein the false priest, "yet the Christian God is causing our people many problems. It's said there are some among the Danes who have joined these heathens who for some odd reason worship a God that was murdered. It's known that for some time the Saxons and Franks have fallen into this error and now the wise worry that such goings-on might come in Swede Mark and here too."

"I will kill any man who becomes a Christian," the King said in heat as his fist pounded the table, "not only would I kill any man who does something that low, no, I will sell his wife to a brothel and his children into slavery. Let no man say that I fail in any way to honor the Gods of my ancestors."

"The Gods know of your devotion, King Hopp, which is one of the reasons that we are here; for only those who are worthy of the Gods can hear what we have to tell you." At his point, all were on edge as they listened intently to Stein who made them wait a little longer as he waited for the drinking horns to be replenished.

"It has been decided that another temple be built to honor the Gods and to serve as a rallying point for the faithful in our battle against the Christian God. We plan to build this temple just north of you in Yingulmarken next year. And when the temple opens it is our intention to have it under the control of several of the worthiest families which of course includes you. This temple will be devoted to the worship of Freya, the Goddess of hearth and home. We have so many dedicated to the God of Thunder and Odin that we have neglected this very important God and that must be rectified."

The King readily conceded that the Goddess had not gotten her fair share of the credit however in a warrior society the Gods who did the fighting would be naturally looked to. Furthermore, he said that he would do all within his power to further the building of this temple. If the priests wanted to construct the wall out of Christian skulls, for example, he would be happy to contribute his share.

"I don't think skulls would befit a shrine to the Mother God," coughed the false priest, "but I admire your sentiments concerning Christians. But what we need more than anything is money to pay for the adornments. You're a man of great wealth, so your neighbors say, so I think that a thousand gold thalers would be sufficient."

The shock of that statement was enough to make King Shortlegs, who would have trouble in raising even half the amount, was so great that some of the men had to turn aside lest they start laughing. The King, it was related afterward, looked like a duck hit over the head by a stone. At this point, Stein was interrupted by a colleague of his who pulled his sleeve and whispered something in his ear.

"As my friend points out there is another way that you can contribute something worthy of your standing. Do you have a daughter who is young and unmarried? Yes?" Seeing a nod from the still stunned King he continued, "It is our intent to have the temple of Freya maintained by women only as is proper, we require suitable candidates to spend a few months with us at Uppsala to learn their duties and then themselves train young maids for their temple duties. I think if you were to let us take her back with us, she could be returned to you as soon as the ice breaks. She would take her servants along with her of course for the sake of propriety; what say you?"

"Well," stammered the King who was so flustered he could scarcely talk, "I cannot dictate something so important without her consent; she would have to agree to it!" This was said in the midst of his mental confusion where the only clear thought was to do anything but bankrupt his kingdom.

"This is fair, Good King Hopp, let her be sent for now so that we can settle this matter. Unless of course, you wish to simply give us a gift of gold." The King then ordered a servant to get his daughter as he attempted to gather his wits by drinking another horn of strong wine. If she refused, he had no idea of what to do. He couldn't very well have the priests taken out and hung, could he?

Thora was in her quarters however this situation was not entirely a surprise to her as Ragnar's trusted childhood friend Hettin had by this time already advised Thora as to what was happening, having first proposed marriage to Thora's serving woman who wasted no time in accepting; for such an offer from a young man who was handsome and a companion of a Prince already famous would enable her to live a better life in a place other than the backwater that she presently lived in and heartily detested.

Once inside the hall, she was apprised of the situation by her father who put the matter before her clumsily, but accurately. He could not openly admit that the gold demanded by the priests would ruin him forever but nonetheless, she got the message.

The skill of the ancient Thespians had never advanced very far into the north but nonetheless Thora gave a beautiful performance of a daughter agreeing to undertake a disagreeable task in order to spare a parent from a dire fate. Her performance was especially agreeable to the large sailor in the rear with the painted face. It was then agreed that in the morning she would depart for the temple at Uppsala with her servants much to the relief of her father. She hugged him dramatically and gave a heartfelt speech at how much she would miss him which brought tears to the King's eyes so much so that he required even more wine.

That was the last that King Shortlegs saw of his beautiful daughter for quite some time for by the time he arose the next morning the sun was high in the sky and the harbor empty. He went over the events of the previous evening having a niggling feeling that something wasn't right. While he couldn't lay a finger on the cause he thought that perhaps something was awry.

His feeling was confirmed a month later when he received a message from King Sigurd of the Danes thanking him for sending his daughter to them! Then by degrees, he began to see the deception that was practiced on him and felt a very much a fool. Even worse was that King Sigurdson expected him to pay the dowry that he had originally promised! For days he fulminated against King Sigurdson and the miserable deception that had tricked him into playing the fool. But no matter how often or how hard he stomped his foot in a confounded rage the deed was done and

his daughter the wife of Prince Ragnar. After days of rage and much wine imbibed, he concluded that he had the best pay the dowry and be done with it for his reputation would suffer more if that were possible if he reneged on his promise.

Later he received word from his daughter that she was with child and if it was the boy, she would name him after him, if it was a girl, she would name her Torlaug after her departed mother. This did much to mollify the old King, so much so that he made a trip to Zealand where he was hospitably welcomed by King Sigurd. The two rulers got very drunk one night and both heartily laughed at the deception of Ragnar and praised his imagination that would no doubt serve him well in the future.

In the fullness of time, Ragnar Sigurdson would be known as Ragnar Lothbrok, a famous Sea-King, but that is a saga for another time. For now, we must leave the Prince of the Danes and his new family in a period of peace and contentment; a time that he would recall happily to the end of his days.

Chapter Fifteen

The Werewolf

Eyestein & Gunnar Answer the Call

In the days before King Harald Finehair imposed his will upon the Norwegian people to become the first High King, there were a number of petty kings who ruled various parts of the realm. Among them was King Rugalf Gardsson of the western realm of Sogn whose throne was in the town of Varlaug, the largest habitation in his realm boasting nearly a thousand residents.

The people were generally unhappy about their lot in life which gave them unending toil besides the threat of famine, disease, accidents, and most of all, death by sword, axe, or arrow. In other words, they were very much like the rest of the Norse during that unredeemed time. But as there was no way to change any of this the people simply shrugged their shoulders, swore to the Gods, and made their way through life as best as they could.

There was little in the way of crime in King Gardsson's realm other than occasional petty theft which earned the culprits a good whipping and a month's forced labor. Revenge killing was not often seen among the lowly or the high for that matter because people understood that once a vendetta is started it could go on until all the combatants and their families, down to the family dog, were dead. So, life went on with little change from one generation to the next.

As for the King, he was enjoying the freedom that comes with losing a shrewish wife to the plague and having little to do other than eat, drink, and play under the sheets with his housemaids. Over time his short but muscular physique had become quite stout from lack of exercise and very grey in his beard; in other words, he was hardly an inspiring sight but so long as his taxes were not too burdensome, he was mostly ignored by his subjects.

The month of Goa is one that is filled with hope for although the weather was still bitter cold the longer days did much to lift the people from out of the deep winter doldrums that forced inactivity can lead to. For Olvindi Karlsson, who lived with his wife just outside the town, spring couldn't come quick enough for he had almost exhausted his share of the Flemish wine that he got from a successful raid during the past summer. He found the taste very agreeable and couldn't seem to get enough of it so much so he was in a stupor when his wife shook him awake as they lay on the rude pallet that formed their bed. She told them that there was a disturbance among the goats in the barn; perhaps a wolf or maybe even a bear come down from the hills. Once he was awake, he wasted no time in getting heavy clothes on and grabbing his trusty axe; he then opened the door and sallied forth ready to kill or drive off any predator.

His wife went back to sleep only to be awakened by his return to bed. As they lay there next to each other he put his arm around her; she welcomed this show of affection by grasping his hand. She didn't realize she thought to herself, how hairy he'd become of late, nor had she noticed how much his nails needed trimming.

At the neighboring farm of Turf Torbindson and his wife Esa Solcersdottar were awakened just past the hour of the owl by the sound of somebody attempting to rip their door from off its hinges. This caused the man to feel a fright in his bowels as if somebody had walked over his grave. In the near-total darkness, he grabbed an oaken club with a spike at the end of it from the corner while his wife threw kindling wood on the fire. By the flickering light, she retrieved a long-curved knife from its home in the rafters and held it in front of her as they stood together waiting for the door to come down. It soon fell with a terrific crash but not before a loud and tailing howl of a wolf was heard which caused the couple to look in fright at each other with bulging eyes. This was followed minutes later by even louder howling which the farmer and his wife were not able to hear, however.

Four days after the howls were heard at night King Rugalf had visitors in his hall which was unusual at this time of year with snow on the ground and ice in the fjords.

The King's chief retainer Jarl Snorri Tavenson, summed up for his employer the reports made to him that day.

"The farms attacked were located on the old mountain trail; why that should be I don't know, nobody goes there."

"Well, *somebody* must use it, or it wouldn't be there would it?" Spoke the King who was rather testy this morning after it was learned that two small farms were attacked, and the residents hideously dismembered and partially eaten.

"Yes, your majesty of course but I can't think of any reason to travel into the mountain pass, especially at this time of year. Even the bears wouldn't go there."

"The bears are hibernating at this time of the year you blockhead," snapped the King as he gulped strong wine in an effort to warm the chilled royal bones, "and they'll stay that way until spring. But do we have any idea who did this and why?"

"None sire," the Jarl said as he quailed under the words of his chief, "the blown snow covered any tracks so it must have happened several days ago. A passing neighbor hauling wood happened to see the door ripped off one of the homes; he summoned others, and they ended up making a search of the nearby farms. If the missing door had not been reported it could have been months before these attacks were found."

"Take horses and men and patrol all the roads outside the town, talk to anyone you meet, and see if they've seen anything unusual. Check those farms that were attacked too, we don't want anyone to be hiding out in them."

The King's mood was not improved when his men later reported to him that a patrol had found signs of another attack. This time it was at the cottage of a solitary woodcutter who lived in a hovel at the edge of wood somewhat beyond where the other attacks took place. No corpse was found however there were definite signs of a struggle with blood freely splashed over everything including the ceiling. It is unknown if this attack took place at the same time as the others or not.

King Rugalf ordered patrols sent through the town and outlying areas at random hours both day and night to look for anything suspicious and interrogate any outsiders. He also had the town cried urging the residents to keep their doors locked and arms at hand. This was all that he could think to do but even as he resumed his usual winter habit of sitting in a cushioned armchair near the fire, he was far from easy in his thinking. He had heard tales of attacks like this before, but they always happened someplace far away. In fact, he thought that they might have been inventions of storytellers. Yet those stories of mayhem had one thing in common he recalled; they didn't stop until the perpetrator was caught and killed. Such thoughts caused him to frown as this situation could, if it got out of hand, seriously impede his winter pastime of merrymaking and wine drinking. He polled his advisors; the few that he had near him at this time of the year; most jarls took the hint from the bears and were dormant in the cold months.

Patrols were duly sent out both day and night and the citizens were advised to take precautions. Life went on albeit slowly and cautiously with nary so much as a mouse showing his nose after dark. The King's words were heeded as folks took extra precautions at night. Stouter beams were being used to bar the doors and previously dull axes and swords now had an edge. Yet the people, as apprehensive as they were about the strange spate of killings were at least hopeful for warmer weather which was improving as the month of Goa faded and Einmanudur had come; already open spots in the river ice flows were seen. Now that a month had passed the people, as well as their ruler, were hopeful that the killer had left the area.

Among those who took precautions to heart was a pair of widows who lived together in a humble cottage on the old mountain track where the murders took place, only they were much closer to the town. Astra, who at age forty was the older of the two, built the fire up each night before retiring and buried within the coals the end of a heavy wrought iron poker. Tofa, the other widow, had a wicked-looking three-sided dagger that she kept under her pillow besides a short-handled boar spear near the entrance. The door was stout and well built by local standards yet on a windy night like this it banged loudly as it was repeatedly buffeted by gusts of wind--but then came a bang without a gust of wind followed by another and another.

Thor Skamilson, a sea captain, and raider who lived with his family within easy sight of the home of the two widows was busy using the piss bucket when a sound on the wind startled him. As soon as he was done with his business he stoked the fire, lit an oil lamp, and had his wife, now awake, help him strap on his armor. Meanwhile, his children hid beneath the covers except for their oldest daughter who grabbed a heavy meat cleaver and stood behind her mother. His actions were none too soon for just then the door staggered from a blow of the kind only a berserker in the heat of battle could deliver. This was followed by more blows loud enough to make the children whimper in fear. Thor, though never daunted within the shield wall, called upon the Gods to help him for help is what he certainly needed. When the door was finally ripped from off its hinges and the bar broken, he was seen crouching down, shield in front of him and spear lowered.

The doleful report of the previous night made its way to the King's hall late the following morning which cast a pall upon the usual jovial activities of the monarch. Heartfelt sorrow for the victims and a generous helping of self-pity caused the old King to writhe in anguish. His minions were dumb when he asked for council; usually it was all that he could do to shut them up. Then suddenly his agitated brain had a thought. He called for his sleigh to be readied and packed with bread, mead, and wine; since tongue-tied mortals have no council perhaps the Gods would have something to say. So, with a small escort, he made his way north of the town to a cottage in the bend of the river where dwelled Emil Sorenson known to all as *Emil the Seer*.

King Rugalf had known the seer for most of his life; even before the man was wounded in battle when the city was besieged years ago. It took a year for him to recover from his wounds and during that time he began to believe that the Gods had chosen him to be a spokesman.

But was he a man of the Gods? Or was he just shrewd in telling people what they wanted to hear? Or just another madman? The King wasn't sure, but he knew for a certainty that the man in question truly believed that the Gods spoke to him.

In a short time, they were at the seer's home which had a forbidding aspect seeing as it was decorated inside and out with the skulls of birds and animals.

"Come in my old friend, I've been waiting for you," said the old man who opened the door as soon as the King pulled up, "have a chair next to the fire so sit and be warmed. You brought me mead and fresh bread, and wine! That's very kind of you; in fact, let's have a horn of wine right now."

This of course the King couldn't refuse; soon they were seated around a central fire pit that glowed with heat and put enough smoke into the air to make their eyes itch.

"Do you know why I have come?" asked the ruler speaking in the informal manner of old friends.

"Yes, of course. I knew that something out of the ordinary was going on for I heard the cry of the wolf a month ago during the night of the full moon and as you know we haven't had a wolf in these parts for many, many years. It was louder last night; he's gotten closer. At daybreak this morning I heard the calls of ravens, so I went out to look and I saw two of them aloft talking to each other; they were no doubt Hugin and Muginn on a mission to find something out for Odin. Apparently, the

One-Eyed Dreamer is taking an interest in us, such an interest, my friend, is very unusual since the violence of this sort is usually too paltry an affair to merit his interest. And now you come to me with the sorrow of murder on your face, all this fills me with dread."

"What does this mean? We've always had killings, too many in my opinion, but why such savage attacks? What purpose do they serve?" Asked the King as he stroked his beard.

"Purpose? The rending and tearing is its purpose," the old seer said as he pulled back the hood of his black cloak to reveal a bushy head of white hair, "There is a savage and malevolent spirit at work here. But the Gods have said nothing to me so far, but one needs not to be a reader of signs and portents to know that a bestial creature is in our midst."

"Too bad," the King sighed as he broke a twig and threw it into the fire, "I was hoping that the Gods whispered something helpful into your ear last night."

"The only thing that I heard in my bed was a howl of triumph. He is nearby, my King, but it will take time for him to gather his energy to strike again and too he must wait on the light of the full moon to give him strength."

"So, 'tis no accident that both attacks happened on the night of the full moon?"

"Nay, for I know enough of the old stories to know that we are talking about a werewolf. They say in the tales that this started with a cursed Saxon and is somehow a part of their religion. Why Christians would relish a fiend who rends, and rips people apart isn't mentioned; maybe it's not true. But the sagas agree that when a man is transformed by the full moon into a wolf on two legs, he becomes very powerful with the strength of ten men and ruthless cunning. If a man is bitten and not killed, he will also become one during the next full moon; don't ask me if a woman can become one of these terrible creatures, I don't know. But so far, we are fortunate that all the victims are dead, or we'd have others; one is bad enough."

Werewolves; the curse of the Saxons

"We don't know for sure if everyone attacked is accounted for. But I'll order every house in the city and the outlying areas searched and we'll question every man. Maybe he will reveal himself in some way. By the hammer, I hope so!"

"One can hope but the man might not even know that he committed these acts of madness. For him, it might have been just a bad dream or nothing at all. You will have to catch him in the act and chop his head off; no matter how strong or savage he is he won't get far without his head."

"But where did he come from?" asked the King plaintively, at this time of the year we don't get visitors unless they come up the frozen river."

"Who can say? But he might not have come here from afar; he could be the victim of a curse. Perhaps a charm or idol that was just biding its time until it awakened," the seer said after a few moments of reflection, "but if what I say is true, we'll know it during the next full moon."

"By the hammer, I hope you are wrong," said the King with a groan, "but I don't have that many men here at this time of year nor will I until the river opens. It's too bad that we no longer have heroes as in the days of yore."

"By the All-Father's big balls, you've got quite a problem on your hands," the seer said between gulps of beer, "but Odin has taken note of this. Perhaps there is more to be learned." At this, he got up and took a small bag from a hook on the wall and dumped its contents on a nearby table. They were obviously knuckle bones, most likely of foxes. After shaking them in his hands he threw them on the table looking intently at the result. Twice more he cast the bones before putting the bones back in the sack.

"The Gods often talk in riddles so that only the wise will know what they mean; in this case it makes me wish that I had more wisdom. They say that help comes from both near and far, but it comes nine days too late to save the next victims."

"So, we must wait until help arrives; until then we're on our own."

"Yes, that is what the Gods say," the seer said as he turned his gaze from the bones to meet the King's eye, "but for what it's worth I will stand by you now just as I stood in the shield wall with you many years ago. But there is one thing that you can do," the older man said as they rose, "I would offer a rich reward for help. Not only offer it here but send messengers near and far to spread the word. I don't know if there are any great heroes left in this world, they were few enough in number even in the olden times, but mayhap one can be found. And of course, it costs nothing to put the word out."

With this, the two men embraced, and the King took his leave. After the old seer stood watching his friend disappear down the road he returned inside; then he took his sword, an ancient blade passed down from his ancestors, from out of its oiled scabbard and tested the blade with his thumb. Odin might send help, or he might not but regardless of any possible actions of the One-Eyed Dreamer, it was prudent to be prepared.

The King took steps too; he sent his men out in groups to search every lodging in the city and to talk to all residents. What exactly they were looking for was unclear, but the men were to report anything unusual no matter how insignificant to their superiors.

By now people had figured out on their own that both attacks happened during the full moon so naturally, there was great worry and apprehension as the next full moon approached; the King proclaimed that the people must band together that night to find safety in numbers. Those who had homes large enough must invite their friends and neighbors over that night; those with nowhere to go could find shelter in the King's great hall or in the Temple of the Gods. He himself would lead a troop of heavily armed warriors through the streets that night; more than that he couldn't do. He had appealed to the Gods for help and did all else that he could think of doing; he could only hope that this foul killer had moved on to greener pastures or would make the foolish attempt to attack his warriors for the King was of the opinion that no beast, even one of supernatural origin, was immune to a quiver full of arrows or the bite of an axe.

When the fell night came the weather had greatly improved but the streets in the lower part of the town, which were now mere pathways of partly frozen mud and the remnants of snow, had become downright treacherous. True, there was a gentle sea wind that wafted welcomed fresh breezes to help blow away the stale smell of winter but tonight the inhabitants of Varlaug had other things in mind as they grouped together in homes bright with fires and weapons close at hand for this was the day of the full moon or, as some men styled it, *the night of the wolf*.

The King, who necessity had motivated to great heights of activity (which he roundly cursed), sat on horseback with several members of his household guard on the rise that his hall was built on while another troop of warriors patrolled the deserted streets. The moon was indeed rising but so far had only shown fitfully through the overcast; then suddenly the clouds parted, and the moon shone forth bathing the buildings in the light of her resplendent glory; soon after came a savage howl that sent shivers up every spine. Men looked at each other through wide eyes; some drew hammer-shaped amulets from around their necks and kissed them; the King stood in his stirrups as he tried to tell where the sound had come from. Then came another sharp and bestial cry that echoed through the town; it seemed to come from everywhere. Drawing his sword and holding it up the King motioned his men to follow him down into the streets.

The Smith

While the King and his minions were patrolling the town's streets his subjects gathered in the larger homes of their more affluent neighbors.

Those who were present in the home of the raider and horse trader Torvalder Ornson included, besides his wife and two girls, several people who for one reason or another didn't think that they stood any chance of living if caught by this bloodthirsty demon on their own. These included an elderly couple that lived nearby; a wagon builder and his son who was simple; and a solitary smith. Besides these, there was a male slave owned by the trader who they simply referred to as a contemptible Skraeling meaning a lowborn stinkard. It was thought that any unsavory beast that attacked would be repelled by the manhood present supplemented by women with torches and butcher knives. The host who thought it best to appear generous that night broke into his store of wine and mead which he shared liberally with his quests except for the slave who only got water. This loosened the tongues of his guests who were forced by circumstances to stay awake long after their usual bedtime. All were gathered around the central fire pit except for one daughter sick with stomach issues who was resting quietly under layers of old blankets in the corner and the slave who sat on the floor opposite her.

At one point their host opened the door to let some fresh air into the stuffy and smoke-filled house and stood outside keeping watch while others either relieved themselves or shuffled about in the gloom trying to get the blood flowing in their legs. As the homeowner stood ready with sword and shield in hand the light of the full moon broke free of the clouds that obscured it earlier. The moon's rays immediately bathed everyone in her abundant light that at other times would have been considered beautiful.

Raven Egilson, the smith, the last to leave, stood in the doorway and like the others raised his eyes to view the sudden flood of moonlight; but when he lowered his gaze his eyes were glazed over and glowing like coals in the fire. As those in front of him were busy filling their lungs with clean air and emptying their bladders he began to tremble as curious physiological changes rapidly overtook him. Within seconds his four canine teeth had grown several inches longer and irregular tufts of hair shot out of his skin especially on his face, arms, and hands. No longer a smith or even a man he lurched out the door unnoticed to those in front of him; but when his host turned around to go back inside the transformed smith slashed his windpipe with inhuman speed and strength.

By now there was very little left to suggest that only moments ago he was just another artisan with big muscles and limited intellect. But the blood that dripped from his claws that had taken the place fingernails was only a small part of his now grotesquely deformed body. His face was matted with thick unruly hair and terrifying protruding teeth; even his ears, now pointed, had grown to twice their normal size.

The others didn't fare much better; the beauty of the moon's rays upon the crisp white snow had now become red botches of horror. Only the girl survived, and she was close to death; the bodies of these victims, the ones they found, were torn and slashed and tossed about.

The King heard this bestial cry of rage and came riding down into the town hoping to catch this fiendish killer; the other patrol group opposite him made the same decision. Splashing half-frozen mud from the horse's hoofs as they rode, they scoured the streets giving hard looks to the land between houses. One man turned his horse around and rode back to where he thought he saw some movement in some bushes; this unwise decision to go it alone was costly. His body, minus one leg, was found in the crook of an apple tree. When morning finally did arrive, they found his missing leg chewed to the bone alongside the main road leading north.

The butcher's bill for that evening was fearful including a slave that had been killed and hauled off in triumph; the sole survivor was a sickly young girl who was covered with the blood of her parents. Everyone was in despair; nobody could think what to do; some began to pack their goods to leave for by now the ice on the river and fjord was almost gone. Even the King had more than once thought about abandoning the town and moving his seat of government somewhere else. But he realized that it might not be possible for him to run away from this horror because the culprit was probably one of his own people.

This failure to apprehend the brutal killer weighed heavy on the ruler so much that not even drink could lift his spirits; his beloved wine from the Flemings tasted like ashes in his mouth. The gloom that afflicted the King's great hall was palpable but perhaps the Gods didn't desert the King for on the ninth day following this most recent attack word was brought to him that two strangers had come from afar to test their mettle against his spawn of evil that had tormented his people. Both names were known to him and did much to rid him of the pessimism that overtook him; indeed, it brought the first smile to his face in a long time. He then filled up his cup as he changed into something more suitable to wear when receiving distinguished visitors for *Eyestein the Far Traveled* and *Gunnar the Bald* had come to the King's hall in the fair City of Varlaug the capital of Sogn.

As the king was busy with his guests the smith was back at this trade making everything from nails to buckles to horseshoes. Always a taciturn man he had been much quieter than usual during the last few months as repeated dark dreams haunted his slumber. Nor were his torments confined to his sleep for even in his waking hours he was not free from apprehensions and strange fancies; indeed, sometimes he felt like he was sleepwalking or living out a daydream. But the worst feeling of all was his constant fear of being watched or being spied upon by unknown enemies.

Nine days ago, he woke up in the morning amongst the logs in his woodpile covered with blood. Inside his house, the fire had gone completely out but he managed to get some embers from his forge to relight it. It was hours before he felt unthawed enough to heat some water to wash the blood from off his body. Again and again, he tried to recall what had happened yet only vague, but frightening, images came to mind.

He put on a clean tunic and jerkin then threw his filthy clothing into a washtub in the rear of his house with a piece of lye soap. While filling it with water it seemed to him that there was once a woman, an old one with a hooked nose, who would come every week to do his wash. But the last he remembered about her was that for some reason he had taken her broken body and threw it down the riverbank into the frozen water below where it laid looking like a child's rag doll all twisted-up in the snow. By now it probably had been washed down the river. It seemed like a foolish thing to do since he now had to do his wash he thought as he dumped a pot of boiling water into the tub.

He knew that something was wrong with him; he didn't always have a mind fogged and addled. Perhaps he should ask a healer for help, yet an instinct told him that this would be very dangerous. His current condition brought to light an old memory; an unpleasant one that he would never forget no matter what his mental state. Indeed, it was something that he would have given anything to see removed from his mind.

He was only a boy walking with his parents through a mountain pass on their way to a newly rented farm when they were attacked. He saw very little of it just a jumble of moving figures and cries. He remembered his father striking down at something with the loud yell of a warrior calling upon Thor followed by the scream of his mother.

The next thing he knew he was being tended by kindly strangers who came upon this grim scene of which he was the sole survivor. He had been flung against a tree after his shoulder was bitten by some unimaginable creature. The rank smell and terrible bestial sound of roaring with glimpses of a dark and hairy figure were the last things he recalled before being thrown through the air so there was little that he could say about what took place.

For the next few weeks, he was very sick alternating between chills and fever; there was also a strange delirium in which he repeatedly heard wolf cries and people screaming. His wound was infected festering day after day until he was at the point of death. But then he began to rally to the amazement of the couple who cared for him. For years he stayed with them until he was ready to go out on his own. The man taught him his trade that he would later excel at, yet he never forgot the day of the attack that killed his family nor the evil dreams and imaginings that seared his soul, but life moved on; he married a local woman when he came to Sogn becoming in time a respected tradesman. Later when she died in childbirth along with her baby, he withdrew from the world concentrating only on his work.

But then strange hallucinations that he suffered after being bitten in that attack years earlier returned with a vengeance; yet he could make no sense out of his recent life, so he stayed quiet, kept his head down trying his best not to attract attention. But as he beat the recalcitrant lumps of melted ore into the items that were at this time of the year in high demand, he fancied that he could hear a wolf howling in the distance getting closer each day.

Eyestein the Far Traveled & Gunnar the Bald

Eyestein Vestarson, born a Swede, had reached thirty-five years of age by which time he had seen more of this world than any living man of the north. He had traveled as a youth with his father on trade missions east to the Rus then later south where he worked as a soldier among the elite guards of Emperor Leo V, *The Armenian*. Then he went further west into Italy where he mixed among the Christians as a merchant where he found it politic to become a follower of Christ. However, he laughed up his sleeve by wearing outwardly a silver crucifix while wearing a small replica of Thor's hammer under his shirt. As a merchant, he traveled to

North Africa and then to the Island of Malta where he settled for a time with a local woman. However, a spurned suitor killed her and wounded him; he was then forced into hiding later taking a ship to Frankia where he traveled north into the land of the Germans finally ending up among the Danes where he lived for several years. More recently he had become a trader, this time with his home in Agder, a Kingdom on the southern tip of Norway.

As for Gunnar the bald, who some called Gunnar the bold, he was a more mysterious character of unknown age; his bald head and traces of grey in his beard belied his energetic manner. He looked to be physically powerful with longer than average arms; he was a carver of runes by trade and more than one person of rank claimed that he held mysterious magical powers that gave him supernatural abilities. The King hoped that these rumors were true because mere talents of the ordinary sort were so far unequal to the task.

"Hail King Rugalf by whose mighty hand are the just rewarded and evildoers punished," said the bald and gangly looking man, "may the hospitality of his hall ever increase."

"Hail Rugalf, the undisputed King of Sogn," said the second man of middling height, red beard, and distinguished bearing, "let his enemies fear him and his friends relish his company."

"Hail Gunnar the bald, I scarce need to ask which of you is he." Here they laughed especially the bald man who thought the jest was apt.

"True enough my King," the man sniggered, "but I think with my iron cap on few will notice; we've come to claim your treasure for ridding you of this beast who slaughters families and rends warriors.

"And you," said the King turning to the other man, "must be Eyestein the Far Traveled. Your fame has reached every kingdom in the land. It cheers me to see you both come to claim my bounty but first you must slay the beast which is what other warriors, some veterans of famous battles, were not able to do."

"It's said you have a werewolf among you; if that is the case we have hard work ahead of us," said Eyestein taking a cup of mead from a servant, "but they have been slain before by others; unfortunately, only after they killed a great many. We intend to use what others have found out, at great cost I've heard, to our advantage. But first, we must see where this beast has attacked and the lay of the land, then we can formulate a plan."

"My men and I will show you where these murders took place; let me call for horses, in the meantime, we have time for a bit more to drink."

For the next few hours, the King and his guests traveled through the streets where the visitors were shown where the attacks took place. Although the snow had melted washing away the gore from these sites it was nonetheless a painful experience for everyone. By the time that they returned to the King's hall all of them had a grim but resolute look on their faces. Of course, word had gone out that famous warriors had arrived from afar to slay the beast and claim the King's reward.

"But tell me how you happened to be in these parts?" asked the King as he looked at Gunnar who was making serious inroads on the ruler's roast pork, "last I heard you were in Gotland."

"My work there was finished," Gunnar replied hoping that this line of inquiry wouldn't be pursued because he left under a cloud due to mischief involving a jarl's daughter, "so I decided to visit my good friend Eyestein in Agder, I hadn't seen him in years."

"He hadn't been with me a week when a storm blew a merchant ship into the harbor," said Eyestein who was not far behind his companion in putting away large amounts of food and drink, "from those on board we heard of the terrible doings here in Sogn and the reward offered to anyone who could end it."

"What do you know about these creatures?" asked the King looking hard at both Gunnar and Eyestein, "everyone I talk to has a different story as to where they come from. Some say they are creatures made by the Christians; others claim it's the work of evil magicians. But what do you say?"

"I've heard the same stories; the blame is always put on those far away; usually among those, we don't like" said Gunnar, "But in this case, the fishwives might be right for according to my friend and fellow rune cutter, Gudgaest Ox-Back of Zealand, they came here long ago from the lands above the Black Sea. How he knows this he didn't say but he never gives out incorrect information. According to Gudgaest, also known as Gudgaest Hammer-Hand, in the mid-summer as the people in that remote land were celebrating a festival in honor of local Gods a ball of fire came across the sky at sunset and burst into flame with the sound of Thor's hammer so close to them that they almost jumped out of their skins in fright. After some thought, they took this as a sign that the Gods approved of their celebration and sent this as a way of letting them know their worship had been heard. The next day they found bits of colorful pieces of metal that they gathered to commemorate the festival but almost every person who gathered them became sick with symptoms unusual for those parts."

"You mean one of those streaking balls that we sometimes see at night rained fire down on the people below. Is that what you say?"

"Yes, my King, exactly that. The ones who gathered up these bits that I think we're from another world or some part of the demonstadt had their hair fall out, their bowels fill with water, their skin fall away and when the fever overtook them just before death, they spat out their teeth. It was like no other disease ever seen. But two people, brothers, survived somehow but on the next full moon they had a violent reaction being transformed into hairy man-like wolves of inhuman strength who slaughtered others without pity or remorse. This happened every time the moon was full; when people understood what was going on they sought to kill the two brothers who escaped just in time on a ship headed for a Saxon port just west of the land of the Jutes. Of course, this led to more people becoming infected with the curse which was blamed on the Saxons; the word *werewolf* is of Saxon origin."

"Very true, friend Gunnar," said Eyestein, "for the few men who had been bitten and survived these attacks became wolves themselves during the full moon and thus the contagion was spread to others. One very cruel element of this is that if a boy was bitten, women could be immune I've heard, they would not immediately become beasts at the coming of the next full moon; only after a passage of years would they turn; in fact, some never turned at all before they died of other causes. Do you know, your highness, if anyone survived after being bit?"

"All that we've found so far were dead," the King said as he stroked his beard in thought, "but there is no way to know for sure if all the victims are accounted for. There could have been others; especially on the farms in the outlying areas. But tell me, my friends, have you hit upon a way of finding this creature? Will you be able to track it to its lair?"

"Maybe first we will have to consult the Gods," said Gunnar.

"The Gods hinted to our seer that you might arrive," allowed the King, "but usually the Gods are not interested in helping us."

"We have some ideas of what might be done but tonight we must fill our bellies and drink your mead. There is time before the moon fully favors us with her light; before then I predict that we'll track this fell creature down."

"You bring us cheer which is something we haven't had in quite some time. Let's drink together then and hope that the All-Father smiles on your efforts."

The next morning as the two guests ate their porridge at the King's table a messenger brought the news that a body, terribly mutilated, had been found resting on a sandbar a few miles downstream by a fisherman; soon everyone was mounted heading for the river trail that led out of town.

One look at the body of this unfortunate woman brought home the truth of what the fisherman said about her condition. Most of her face had been ripped apart in a savage way very similar to previous attacks. How long she had been dead was impossible to say but it wasn't recent.

"She could have been dead a month or more; there's no way to know. But we know she wasn't a farmer's wife; look at her clothing; no, she was a woman who lived here in the town," said Eyestein sadly as he viewed the pathetic remains before him, "have any women been reported missing?"

"No, not that I know of," replied the King after some thought, "but I'll send some men out when we get back to the hall; they can canvass the town and see if anyone is missing."

"We'll go with them," said Gunnar as he mounted his horse, "we need to hear what the people are saying; there have to be clues somewhere if we have the luck to find them."

"Sound thinking," the King replied as he led them forward at a trot, "we need to know who this woman was if we can." He also said that he would have this woman's body taken to a suitable place to be burned and the ashes placed in the burial grounds.

That afternoon they spent with the King's trusted retainers as they canvassed the town for hours asking if any women were missing which turned out to be a difficult task as a number of them were thought to have left because of the recent mayhem; just about everyone had a friend or a relative living on one of the surrounding farms of which there were hundreds. But the absence of one woman; an older widow of about forty years of age was thought by those who knew her as suspicious. She had said nothing to anyone about leaving and considering her meager circumstances, she washed clothing for a living, which made it unlikely for her to flee to the countryside as others did. It was noted too that she lived hard by where the other known victims lived. This didn't shed any light on the situation, but it did cause the two hunters, as the people called them, to wonder why this particular victim had been taken elsewhere to be disposed of. Eyestein went so far as to declare, as they rode back to the hall, that this might be the key to finding out where the beast might be found.

"Well," said Gunnar whose stomach was reminding him of how hungry he was, "it's obvious that we have a changeling here; in other words, a genuine werewolf who is active only in the light of the full moon: it seems too that he probably lives in the area in which the attacks occurred which rules out a great deal of the town. But by now he must know that he's being sought."

"He might not even be aware of it. It's possible that he doesn't remember what he has done when he resumes his human shape."

"Shrewd observation my friend Eyestein, but there is just no way to know at present. All we can say with certainty is that he either came from another place and arrived sometime previous to the first attack or that he was bitten as a child and the curse is only now manifesting itself. That being the case we can rule out women of course who are not susceptible to becoming a ravening killer and likewise we can say that it is not a child and probably not an old man. No, I think we are looking for a man fit of wind and limb."

"We need to investigate this woman further in the morning and be quick about it," Said Gunnar as they neared the King's hall, "we must start in the morning early."

"You'll get no argument from me," replied the famous traveler, "the King thinks that we have some formula for killing the wolf so we need to come up with something; we have only two weeks before the next outbreak and the King expects us to nail the hide of that creature to the door of his hall; if we let him down it will be OUR hides on that door."

To this unpleasant observation Gunnar could make no reply but concluded that there was no use in fretting over something at this time of day; not when the King's pork and mead were so close at hand.

Astrid Audunsdottar

True to Eyestein's advice the two men were on the move early the next day intending to learn what they could about the savage death of an unknown woman whose body had been found just downstream from the town. In particular, they wished to enquire about the disappearance of a woman who lived in the vicinity.

These questions soon yielded some information. An ancient couple, both of whom had seen over fifty winters, claimed to know her well.

"Her name was Astrid, I remember her father, Audun, who was known as Audun Halfhand, and her mother Hildi. He was a leatherworker and yes, sometimes he raided. Astrid was their youngest child, she married a man from somewhere north of here, but he went raiding and drowned in a storm, later she married a farmer, but he died too, the plague, I think. She did wash for people, but I don't know all she served but I can take you around to some of them. But no, I haven't seen her in quite some time; I can show you where she lived, you'll never find it on your own."

True to his work the man, whose bald pate was almost a match for Gunnar's, took them to where she lived as it was close by. He certainly told the truth about them not finding it on their own for it was hidden behind the growth of rowan bushes.

The dwelling was a humble cottage whose bare interior bespoke of the poverty of the one who lived there. Beyond a few articles of clothing and kitchen utensils, there was little to be seen; it looked like it had been deserted for some time as the droppings of small animals were seen.

Then the old man led them to the home of the smith which was only a few yards away. He was easy enough to find; all one had to do was follow the sound of his hammer which led them to his forge situated under a large tree on the side of his home. At the moment he was busy hammering out a long scythe blade but when he saw the men approaching, he put aside his hammer. The horses became restive as they neared him, no doubt from the smell of the forge, so Eyestein thought anyway.

The smith was exactly what one would expect to see engaged in this trade. He was a burly man who wore a long leather apron, upon his hands and arms were seen many scars no doubt the result of working for years with sharp blades and hot irons. The smoke had affected his eyes too for they looked to be swollen with irritation and watery. Gunnar also saw scars on his neck that made him think that this man had gone raiding which was of course common enough.

The old man told them previously that the smith was single but couldn't recall if he was ever married or not; all he could say was that he had a sound reputation as far as his trade went but otherwise was the solitary sort

When asked about his neighbor he said that he hadn't seen or heard from her for quite a while and had to do his own wash. No, he didn't have any idea of where she went or when she might return but he'd heard of the attacks. No, he didn't think of looking for her and it wouldn't have done any good to go to her cottage. Gunnar tried to pry more out of the man who seemed out of his depth when questioned about anything other than horseshoes and the cost of nails. But as they were leaving, he looked hard at Gunnar and said, "The wolf will always kill the rascals first; by the month of Skerpla he'll get to the honest men. The All-Father might be the enemy of the wolf but when the wolf howls the Gods hide; men should learn from that."

"Did that make sense to you?" Gunnar asked as they walked away from the smith's forge, "He didn't seem to me to be a man interested in the Gods."

"The saga's talk about the wolf Fenrir who will supposedly eat the sun on the last day but I'm not sure how this fellow would know that. But there is nothing clear-cut about how Odin thinks about wolves; after all, he owns two of them."

"If you want to know what the Gods think you must go to the seer, that's what everyone else does." Interjected the old man who overheard their talk. This line of thought was put aside for the moment as they came upon a woman who attempted to sell them a duck and wouldn't take no for an answer. As it turned out she knew Astrid Audunsdottar and in the style of an excessively talkative neighbor gave the men all sorts of useless information. But one fact was gleaned; this woman knew for a fact that the woman had suddenly gone missing; several folks who she did washing for asked about her. But overall, not much was made of a missing washerwoman with all the fear that having a maniacal killer loose engendered. Others confirmed the portrait of this victim as just a humble working woman who got less than her share of luck in this world and suddenly disappeared.

That night when the King asked about their progress that day the two men had little to say beyond noting that they were still gathering information and had no conclusions to make yet. This was just a way of saying that they hadn't made any progress yet. They had hoped to learn more from tracking down the people who knew Astrid Audunsdottar but that hadn't materialized. Or perhaps there was a clue to be found in examining her disappearance, but they lacked the sight to see it. And as Eyestein pointed out that they were only supposing that it was her body that was found. When Gunnar mentioned the strange statement that the smith offered the King suggested that the Gods be, again, consulted. After all, their very appearance had been foretold by the old seer. This met with approval from the men; the King even sent word to the kitchen to prepare a couple of extra loaves and some of his best wine to be sent with them the next morning.

The Seer & the Saxon Silver

The next morning as the two men once more left the King's hall to journey into the town; this time to consult with Emil Sorenson the seer.

They found the old man seated on a bench outside his door in the warming sun, a common practice after a long and dreary winter.

"The King sent you with gifts!" the old man exclaimed as he saw Gunnar take a sack from a bag on his saddle that contained fresh bread and a small crock of butter; he looked even more pleased when he saw Eyestein do the same only in his case it was two large skins of wine.

"We are . . .," started Gunnar only to be cut short by the seer.

"Everyone within fifty leagues of the place knows who you are; the people have talked about nothing else since you got here. Indeed, I am almost as thrilled to see you as I am to get this wine. I think I'll sample it right now."

"We've come . . .," started Eyestein when he too was cut short as the seer took the stopper out of the spout.

"Yes, yes, we know that too. You want to know what the Gods have to say about all of this. But go to the back of the house and fetch something to sit on; no sense sitting inside on a fair day like this."

"This is some of the best bread I've ever tasted," said the old man as he took a bite of fresh buttered bread, "and this wine is good enough to be served at Odin's table I'll warrant. But you'll be wanting to know what the Gods think about our little problem; don't you?"

"Yes, we do. We need to know what to do; the quicker the better. The King has strong feelings about his subjects getting their lungs torn out and their faces eaten." Gunnar said after taking a pull from the wineskin.

"And you two have volunteered to exterminate the beast that will soon be loose amongst us again. Yet you have no idea what to do."

"I don't know if the Gods talk to you or not," said Eyestein with a small smile on his face, "but you are shrewd enough without them no doubt."

"But your words are true enough," Gunnar said as he scratched his bald pate, "yet I think we'll manage somehow. I've always found it prudent to adopt an air of confidence when dealing with a thorny problem; showing weakness or hesitancy in our society is always a bad idea."

"So it is, so it is," laughed the old man, "so what to do, eh? I've heard the old washerwoman is dead; I didn't know her but it's still a sad ending for her, I hope that Loki's daughter will treat her with compassion." To these words, the men readily agreed. This was followed by a long silence as the men chewed on bread and sipped wine.

"So, the curse of the Saxons is upon us," the old man mused as he took a break from chewing on bread, "a man turned into a wolf would be damn hard to kill. Did you bring Thor's hammer with you? It would be much easier if you did."

"No hammer, old friend, but a blade sharp enough to cut his head off." Said Eyestein as he wiped his mouth with his sleeve.

"If he will oblige you by standing still; and if you can find him when the moon shines full again. But have no fear; the All-Father knew you would come here and showed me something. Go inside the door and bring out the sack hanging from the rafters."

"This," said the seer as he took the sack in his hands, "was captured from the priests of the west Saxons. It is the symbol of their murdered God that they have made use of for their magical rites no doubt. You can see here," he said showing them the base of the cross, "where it fits on top of a rod; was carried by one of their chief wizards. My father took this on the day that I was born and when he died, he gave it to me for good luck. Since then, I've had it buried beneath my cabbages; I now give it to you for your need is greater than mine."

"This is generous of you," said Eyestein as he took this solid silver crucifix in his hands marveling at its beauty and weight but a bit uncomfortable about touching this symbol of the heathen Christians, "but I must ask of what use this can be in our present circumstances?"

"Think of the great heroes in song and story; what did they have that you lack? A great weapon! I can't give you an enchanted sword to smite down trolls or a magical cow whose mooing will give you victory, but I can offer you the purest silver to be found anywhere in the north and silver is something that the wolf can't abide. Take this to old Jorkel, the one who makes the King's weapons, and have him make you a spear point. But" he said looking at each of them hard in turn, "strike deep; bury it deep in the heart of this wolf-man; take this with you when you leave, but first, let's drink a bit more."

"May the Spear-Shaker sustain you," said Gunnar, "if only we knew where to look for this fiend. But our hearty thanks to you for this great gift."

"When you see Jorkel ask him if the *huntsman* is still in these parts. He's his cousin and knows a lot about animals. At some point you'll have to get close enough to kill this beast; maybe he can help you with that. As to where this creature is hiding the Gods didn't vouchsafe that information to me, but my instincts tell me he is close. In my mind's eye,

I see him looking at the town as a butcher might look at a flock of sheep. Ever he calculates which person has the sweetest meat and the most wholesome blood. By now the blood lust is growing each day and he trembles in anticipation; in less than two Thor's days from now the moon will shine in her glory; then the beast will roam again. He is stronger now than he was before; with each passing month his hide grows thicker and his muscles stronger. Each time he kills he takes a portion of the victim's life essence for his own; kill him now while you have the chance."

These words of the seer were a caution that the two men couldn't neglect; on their way back to the King's compound they talked about weapons and theoretical methods to kill the beast. Besides tickling him between the ribs with a silver-tipped spear simply hacking off the creature's arms or better yet the head appeared to hold promise. But Eyestein had his doubts pointing out that just the sight of this creature would put fear into the bowels of every berserker in the north; imagine what it would be like to see his bared fangs and feel his heated breath.

"If that doesn't make you shit your pants then you're a brave man." Said Gunnar as the two men exchanged looks.

Goats in the Moonlight

Two weeks later the King sat with his faithful retainers and other notables which of course included Gunnar and Eyestein at an early supper. There was little doubt in the monarch's mind that tonight their strength and nerves would be tested.

"You plan to stick this up the arse of the wolf-man tonight," said the king as he nodded at the spear that stood propped up in a corner, "It's a thing of beauty if you can get him to bend over that is. But why did you go for a short handle? You'll never reach him from horseback."

"Horses would only bolt; any fighting will have to be done on foot," said Gunnar, "I have the long arms though so I'll take the spear, Eyestein will use his *sax*." He said referring to the short-handled axe that the German tribe the Saxons were named after.

"I heard Jorkel had a fit when you told him to make the spear point out of silver," the King said as he ate his plate of roast goose, "and Krause the Wend, my huntsman told me of your plan for tonight; he says it might work but then again perhaps not. Most of my men think you two are crazy."

"The words of your seer have led us to this point," Eyestein remarked as he reached for more goose.

"They think he's crazy too," the King said as the grease dripped from his chin, "he had this wealth while all this time living like a beggar. I think if we survive the night, I'll tell him to come to live here with me. He's getting too old to stay by himself."

"I'm sure the Gods would favor that," said Gunnar as he pushed his plate of bones picked clean away and reached for the mead, "but there is no reason for you to come with us tonight. Kings who lead from behind live longer."

"I fear death from the decrepitude of old age much more; besides I am just too curious as to how your plans will work to stay home."

"You are not alone in your curiosity," said Eyestein, "your hunt master Krause is coming along too. He has the biggest boar spear I've ever seen, but we should get ourselves ready for all must be in place before the moon rises and there is much to do."

The words of the far-traveled man were true enough for by the time the wagons were loaded, the teams of horses hitched and the warriors assembled twilight was upon them.

The people of the town peeked out from behind hedges and the cracks of privy doors to see the strange cavalcade of wagons followed by armed men on the horse; none could imagine what this meant on this of all nights. Those who didn't see the strange procession certainly heard it as the two-dozen nanny goats and kids bleated loudly as they were being hauled down the roadway. Many people had fled to the King's estate for this evening of moonlight while others banded together as they did the last time only with the groups being larger and with more armed men present. While there were a lot fewer people in town the ones who remained couldn't imagine what the purpose of wagons full of caged goats could be.

This was the work of Krause, the man of the Wends (a client tribe of the Saxons); nothing he said, would call louder to a wolf, no matter how many legs, than the sound of domestic animals. The two large wagons containing the animals were parked in the junction of trails close by where the other attacks took place. The horses were taken away as they would no doubt become frantic once they smelled a wolf.

This was of course the bait of the trap; in a nearby stand of stunted trees and bushes, Eyestein and Gunnar waited in the dark. Back further on higher ground the King and his men waited ready to pounce on the beast at the right time. Such was the plan anyway; would it work? Nobody had any idea. The only thing that anyone could say with certainty was that the time dragged intolerably as the men crouched with ears perked to catch the slightest noise.

By midday, the smith had quit his forge and retired to his cabin to rest. He had been feeling increasingly on edge in the last week; today he trembled at intervals and had a thirst that was hard to quench. He felt apprehensive as if something was approaching almost like he was being stalked like an animal in the forest or being spied on by somebody always just out of sight; but what it meant eluded his waking mind. He tried to rest by lying down on his pallet; eventually, he went to sleep but it wasn't the kind that would bring rest to either his body or mind. No, unknown terrors perused him with great vigor in his dreams causing him to writhe in fear and anguish.

When he awoke just after dusk he was bathed in sweat; after he had finished pissing behind the bushes, he noticed that his vision was now tinged with red. Dazed and confused he stumbled about until he suddenly felt so overheated that he tore his clothing off entirely. Then looking up through bulging eyes he caught a glimpse of the powerful rising moon between intermittent clouds. He stared at the beauty of this heavenly queen until he noticed that his hearing, now very sharp, had caught a sound on the wind that his bestial mind identified instantly; a sound that made his senses slaver and eyes bulge. His blood boiled with a primal lust for flesh; unable to restrain himself he let out a savage howl as he bounded in the direction of the sound. Fully on the hunt, he leaped over bushes and hedges until he reached the crossroads; now he could not only hear the kids bleating but the smell of them too which drove him frantic. Soon he was within plain view of two big farm wagons with cages full of goats: tender kids and their fat and soft-skinned mothers.

But then he skidded to a stop as he smelt something else: danger! Others were here too, men. His instincts told him that this was a trap; crouching low he studied the ground in front of him and repeatedly raised his nose to smell the air; yes, they were here but he couldn't see where; then a kid made a loud bleating noise that he found nearly impossible to resist; warily he made his way forward eyes and ears open to every sound. But just as he reached the cages, he heard sounds; the sounds of men running at him full tilt with their weapons ready to strike; with a snarl and short howl he sprang to his left to meet them.

The two warriors reached the man-wolf together; Eyestein in the full panoply of war including his iron helm, held his shield before him with his short-handled axe ready to bite at the first opportunity while Gunnar wearing only a leather jerkin and like his friend a cap of iron held his spear in front of him with both hands. However, both soon found themselves facing the wrong way when the creature simply bounded over their heads landing behind them. Needless to say, this disconcerted the two bounty hunters who nonetheless quickly recovered and changed front. Then the beast with fantastic speed ripped the shield out of Eyestein's hands and beat him over the head with it twice before he was forced by Gunnar's jabs to move away. The man-wolf whose movements were so quick as to be difficult to follow in the moonlight threw the shield at Gunnar and leaped on top of Eyestein dragging him to the ground. For a moment they tussled as Eyestein tried to pull the creature's hands from his throat.

Finding him too hard to strangle the man-wolf pulled back and attempted to rake the warrior's face with his claws. Eyestein showing the quickness of a striking snake snatched a knife from his belt and planted it in the pit of the werewolf's arm which brought forth a quick howl as the beast sprang to its feet. He snarled as he yanked the knife out then tossed it back at Eyestein in a lot less time than it takes to tell about it. The bald master of runes had not been idle during this time but with the beast's quick movements found no opportunity to stab him. With the frenzied killer back on his feet Gunnar repeatedly attempted to stick him with the spear's end but failed.

Eyestein tried to get up but got only a kick in the face for his efforts. Gunnar wasn't doing much better for the creature had grabbed the end of his spear with its hands and was working hard to pull it out of Gunnar's grip. It was then that the desperate Eyestein found his dropped short axe and flung it hitting the beast's ankle; this distracted him enough for Gunnar to move the point of the spear over a few inches at which time he plunged forward for all he was worth. In went the spear tip until several inches of it protruded from out its hairy back; Gunnar now sensing that victory was in sight summoned every ounce of strength to pull the tip out and shove it in again and again until the man-wolf fell backward spewing blood from its mouth. Then Gunnar struck one final time putting the silver spear tip directly in the fallen fiend's heart.

As the men stood there triumphant but out of breath the beast's body started to revert to the human shape which they then recognized as being that of the smith. The body of the man was displayed for several days before it was burned; people marveled at this many walking long distances to view the corpse.

Of course, this victory over the man-wolf was celebrated far and wide firmly establishing Eyestein and Gunnar in the Pantheon of Heroes and demi-gods. The King of Sogn who took full credit for his foresight in hiring these warriors loaded them down with gifts and treasure. Several feasts were held in which the bards competed with each other in the retelling and embellishing of their triumph. Over the ensuing years both men, using intelligence, luck, and bravery, would win more accolades but none were as sweet to them as their first victory.

When the King personally led them to the ship waiting to take them downriver to the ocean, he proclaimed that now that they were free of this malignant curse the kingdom could get back to normal. His people, who were almost all farmers, cheered their King with enthusiasm as they returned once more to walking behind the plow just as their ancestors did for millennia.

Epilogue

The slave who all thought to be dead was still very much alive having survived the painful bite that he received on his upper arm the night in which his owner and his wife had been slaughtered. Being thought dead was a great advantage for an escaped slave; otherwise, he would have been hunted like a wild pig with dogs and men on horses. The pain of the bite was intense and for two days his fever rose alarmingly for one on the run with little more than the clothes on his back. He continued down the river stealing crusts of bread and odd bits of clothing wherever he could. Before being captured and sold into slavery he lived as a thief having been separated from his parents at a young age due to a raid on their farm. If his family survived, he never knew but he suspected they were all killed.

His fever abated as he went south and west towards the salt sea. In fact, he was now relatively safe in this thinly settled part of Sogn. He found a farm long deserted; the shallow graves near the house told him that the former residents had probably died of the plague; this worked to his advantage for people tended to avoid such places as being cursed. As luck would have it, he found a few items that would greatly help him; one being a long thin but still sharp knife; the other a flint and steel to make fire with.

He made a spear out of a thin birch branch that allowed him to spear fish in the nearby shallow river that was ideal for his purpose. Within a few hours, he was sitting in the central fire pit cooking his catch on an open flame. His life had taught him to get by on little so living in this abandoned homestead was no hardship.

He rested here while he regained his strength; how long he was there he wasn't sure since time was of little account to a slave; in fact he no idea of how old he was. He intended to go along the fjord until he found a boat that he could steal. From there he would either sail south to the sea known as Kattegat then east to the land of the Danes or go all the way south where he could find refuge among his kinsmen the Frisians. But as the days passed, he became increasingly uneasy; he looked about repeatedly in order to see if anyone had come to investigate signs of life on the old farm, yet he had heard, seen, and smelled nobody. Even so, to stay there much longer was to invite discovery so he resolved to start his journey toward the sea. A day later he reached the first habitation which was a cottage of a trapper. There were pelts of animals in bundles ready to take to the market, but the owner was out; presumably to check his snares. The former slave helped himself to a leg of rabbit and some bread before stealing his boat. Going by water would be much faster he knew but he had to be watchful; he would have a hard time explaining himself if he was questioned by authorities.

But his luck held, the few boats that he saw were merely farm workers and he was getting closer to the sea; he could smell it in fact. The thought of leaving this land of misery cheered him yet he was far from easy in his mind. He'd been gone a month as of today, but although free of chains he became increasingly agitated as the day went on; by mid-afternoon, he became so confused that he pulled the boat up on shore in a thicket of fir trees and collapsed into a heap where he remained for some hours; when he finally woke, he was bathed in sweat. Pulling himself to his feet he looked through the trees to the neighboring fields where he saw the full moon rising on the horizon.

The nearest farmer and his family were mystified by the unsettling wolf cry that they heard that night. Wolves were not completely unknown, but they seldom came close to human habitation unless driven by starvation which was unlikely at this time due to plentiful herds of deer.

The next morning another farmer found one of his goats ripped apart with bits of hide, bones, and other parts thrown about, some landing in tree branches. He fingered his amulet in fear at the sight of this never knowing how lucky he was not to suffer a similar fate. For although the wolf found the meat of the nanny goat tasty, he had no idea at that time how much sweeter man's flesh would taste. Not until he reached the shores of the Frisians would he learn to drink human blood; the sorrow that he brought to those shores lasted for a generation.

The other survivor of that evening's savage attack was a young girl who had been sick at the time. The blanket that she wore around her shoulders was soaked with blood when she was found; she looked more dead than alive but contrary to expectations she lived. She had received a nasty gash on her neck that became infected, but it wasn't clear if this was a bite or not. If a boy had suffered such a wound, there could have been consequences for nobody wanted a demon to come forth at some unknown future time. But females are not, as the common thinking went, susceptible to being infected with the Saxon curse.

She was adopted by a childless couple who lived on a farm a few miles out of the city. Her new parents treated her well enough but of course, she had to work hard like the rest of them. But she began to dread the rise of the full moon for during such times she had trouble sleeping; often being woken by the cries of distant wolves that only she could hear. Alarming physical changes began to take place; her eyes would glaze over, and she would tremble. Because these took place after everyone else was asleep, they were unaware of what was happening.

When the time came that she should be married her mother found her a good match; a hard-working, even-tempered youth whose parents lived nearby on a farm that they rented. The prospect of marriage excited her for she wanted to have her own hearth and home as much as any other woman, but she secretly wondered why she was different from others and what it meant.

Her marriage cannot be called a success though; in fact, it was hardly a marriage at all. By ill luck her wedding took place on the first night of the full moon; when visitors arrived to see the couple the next day, they were horrified to find that the groom had his throat ripped out and the wedding bed soaked in blood. As for the bride, she disappeared entirely; presumably abducted by whatever foe had perpetrated this outrage. The local jarl investigated the matter to the best of his ability but nothing about this terrible event could be established other than what could be seen with their own eyes. In time the uproar faded away, but it was never entirely forgotten.

But the young woman wasn't abducted; she had in fact fled as soon as she awakened the next morning. She understood what had happened and was tempted to run the blade of a knife into her heart, but her self-preservation instincts overtook her so in the end she took a few articles of clothing, a little money, and left eventually ending up in a port to the west. What happened to her after that is not known but she was never suspected of any deaths by mutilation for as everyone knows a woman cannot become a werewolf.

About the Author

R obert Peterson is a lifelong student of Norse history mythology and genealogy who lives in Florida with his cat Arthur. He was previously a Fellow of medieval literature at Miskatonic University. He is also the author of the *Runemaster of Denmark* series which tells the story of a powerful mage caught up in a world of warfare, intrigue, and oath-breaking. He and his Storm-Queen wife must navigate a world of tumult while holding fast to their own values and beliefs.

Bibliography and Suggested Further Reading

A Translation and Analysis of the Chronicle of Roskilde by Emma Barnett, Reed University, 2010. Written in the mid-12th century it predates a far larger work by Saxo Grammaticus. The author was a church official connected closely with Roskilde Cathedral. The manuscript is written in Latin coving a period starting around 826 C.E. which is the traditional date for the introduction of Christianity in Denmark.

The Anglo-Saxon Chronicle, 1912, translated by the Rev. James Ingram, E. P. Dutton & Co. London. Written in the 9th century by a scribe in Wessex it's the annals of the Saxons from the time of the invasion of Julius Caesar to the reign of Alfred the Great.

The Poetic Edda, The 1908 version by Olive Bray, available online and in many printed forms. The original 13th century author who collected these stories is unknown other than he was probably a high churchman. This work is the most extensive and probably the most reliable of all the early Icelandic and Norse sources. Available online.

The Prose Edda by Snorri Sturluson, 1179-1241, a historian and politician who collected and edited Icelandic Norse mythology and heroic stories from a Christian perspective. His work is open to interpretation, and he has suffered extensively at the hands of modern scholars.

The History of the Danes by Saxo Grammaticus who is thought to have been a 13th century churchman. He gathered folk tales and sagas some of which vary considerably from the Icelandic sources. Eric Christiansen's translation is the most modern. The saga's collected in the Eddas often vary considerably from this source.

A History of the Vikings, Gwyn Jones, Cambridge University Press, too many editions to count. A great book at any level, highly recommended for further reading.

The Saga of the Volsungs, translated and edited by Jackson Crawford. 2017 Hackett Publishing. The author is probably the greatest living scholar on the Old Norse Language and his many lectures available on YouTube are a must for anyone who really wants to understand the old Norse culture.

Egil's Saga, Penguin Classic, 2004. Story of the life and times of Egil Skallagrimsson who a 10th century poet, farmer, warrior, and psychopath. His story is a popular one because he is such a strangely gifted person who had a lot of talent besides some very disturbing personal traits.

Private Papers of Rollo A. Weems. Author's collection. An assortment of essays, primary sources, tertiary notes, papers on mythology and the life of Sir John Borough, GKA.